ANNAJEWEL
A Modern Myth

by

Mitchell Scott

ISBN: 979-8-9944185-0-5

Morning Vale Press

Printed in the United States of America

Chapter 1: The Cradle of the Valley

The valley did not have a name, and that was exactly how Kael liked it. Names belonged on maps, and maps were the first thing armies looked at when they needed grain, or timber, or young men to hold spears.

It was a scoop of green silence carved out of the rugged foothills, invisible from the trade roads that snaked along the gray ridges above. To the rest of the world—a world that groaned under the weight of iron boots and petty warlords—this place simply did not exist.

The surrounding slopes were a snare of trees and heavy brush, land that resisted passage.

Only the southern ridge gave way. There, a deer trail naturally opened toward the nearest road.

Kael moved along the ridge, his breath steaming in the chill morning air. This was the weak point in their armor.

He didn't build a fence here; fences implied ownership. Instead, Kael tended the brambles.

He wore thick leather gauntlets, stained black with old sap. Carefully, methodically, he grabbed the thick, thorny vines of the blackberry bushes and wove them together. He pulled a dead branch across the gap, arranging it to look like it had fallen there in a winter storm years ago.

He stepped back, scanning his work. To a soldier riding past on the high road, looking for a place to water his horse, this didn't look like a homestead. It looked like a choked, impassable ravine.

"Stay small," Kael whispered to the thorns. "Stay small, and the hawk won't see the mouse."

He descended into the green bowl of the valley. The air changed as he dropped in elevation, the dusty, metallic scent of the high road replaced by the smell of damp earth and the sweet, fermenting scent of fallen apples.

The cabin sat near the stream; built of timber Kael had felled himself. They hadn't cleared the forest to build it; they had built it into the forest. The roof was covered in living sod, a thick carpet of moss and grass that, from above, looked like nothing more than a bump in the forest floor.

Kael paused by the stream to wash the sap from his gloves. In a deep, quiet pool near the bank, a trio of spotted trout held their position against the current, their scales flashing pink and silver. They watched Kael with unblinking eyes, unafraid. They knew nothing of nets or hooks.

Inside the cabin, the air was warm and smelled of yeast.

Mara was in the root cellar, the cool, earth-walled pantry dug into the side of the hill behind the kitchen. She moved slowly, one hand resting on the high, tight mound of her stomach, the other checking the seals on the clay jars.

They did not live like kings—kings were wasteful. They lived like squirrels.

The shelves were lined with the wealth of prudence. There were jars of trout Kael had smoked over low hickory fires until they were hard as wood. There were baskets of dried apple rings, brown and shriveled but packed with sugar. There were sacks of acorn flour and bundles of willow bark for fever.

In the village of Oakhaven, five miles away, people were starving. Here, Mara counted every apple. She wasted nothing.

"You're counting again," Kael said softly from the doorway.

Mara turned, a tired smile touching her lips. "I'm checking the winter stock. If the snow comes early..."

"We have enough," Kael promised, stepping down into the cool earth to take the jar from her hands.

"We are three people now, Kael. Or we will be soon."

She pressed her palm briefly to her stomach, as if listening for reassurance.

Kael froze. "Is it time?"

"The pain is faint," she said. "But it is there. Like a whisper."

Kael set the jar down. The calm of the morning evaporated. "I'll go for Elara. Now."

"Take the high path," Mara instructed. "Don't let them see you."

The journey to Oakhaven was a transition from color into grayness.

As Kael crested the ridge and stepped onto the trade road, the vibrancy of the valley died. The trees here were stripped of their lower branches for firewood. The fields lay fallow, choked with brown weeds.

Oakhaven had once been a market town. Now, it was a huddle of survivors. The buildings leaned against each other like tired old men, their slate roofs slick with grime. The town smelled of wet wool, woodsmoke, and exhaustion.

Kael kept his hood up. He walked past a group of mercenaries in rusted chainmail who sat by a trough, sharpening swords. They didn't look at Kael. To them, he was just another peasant.

He found Elara's cottage on the edge of town. Elara was in her garden, pulling turnips. But she wasn't alone.

A young girl, perhaps twelve years old, was struggling to pull a stubborn root from the half-frozen ground. She was thin—too thin, with wrists like bird bones and eyes that looked too big for her face. She wore a shapeless gray tunic that had been patched a dozen times.

"Put your back into it, Nia," Elara barked, not looking up from her own work. "The frost doesn't care if you're tired."

The girl gritted her teeth and heaved, stumbling back as the turnip finally gave way.

"The quiet one returns," Elara said, sensing Kael at the gate. She stood up, wiping dirt from her hands. "Is it today?"

"Soon," Kael said. "She is waiting."

Elara nodded. "Nia! Get the bag. And the heavy cloak. We are walking."

The girl, Nia, dropped the turnip and scrambled toward the cottage. "Yes, Mistress Elara."

"You're bringing the girl?" Kael asked, keeping his voice low.

"My knees are old, woodworker," Elara muttered. "I need young legs to carry the iron. Besides, she needs to learn that babies don't come from cabbage patches."

Nia returned, heaving a heavy leather satchel onto her shoulder. She looked at Kael with nervous curiosity.

"Let's go," Elara commanded. "The air in this town tastes like despair, and I am tired of it."

The return trip was slow. Elara moved with a relentless gait, but Kael found himself slowing his pace for the girl. Nia was struggling under the weight of the bag, her breathing ragged. She stared at the ground, putting one foot in front of the other.

When they finally slipped through the bramble gate and looked down into the valley, the reaction was immediate.

Nia stopped dead. She nearly dropped the bag.

Her eyes went wide, darting from the green grass to the clear water of the stream, and finally resting on the apple trees. To a girl raised in the gray mud of Oakhaven, this wasn't just a valley. It was a myth.

"It's... it's green," she whispered.

Elara swatted her shoulder. "Close your mouth, girl, before a bug flies in. It's just dirt and water." But even Elara took a deep breath, tasting the clean air. "Though it is better dirt than most."

They descended to the cabin. As they approached the porch, Kael saw Nia staring at a basket of apples sitting by the door—

bruised ones, meant for the pigs or the compost. She looked at them the way a starving dog looks at a bone.

Kael stopped. He reached into the basket and picked out the best one—a deep red fruit, slightly soft but sweet. He held it out.

Nia flinched, looking at Elara for permission.

"Take it," Kael said gently. "We have plenty."

Nia took the apple. She didn't wipe it. She bit into it with a ferocity that made Kael's heart ache. Juice ran down her chin, and for a moment, the exhaustion vanished from her face.

"Don't get used to it," Elara warned, though her voice wasn't unkind. "Paradise makes you soft."

For the next three days, the cabin was crowded. Elara slept by the hearth, smelling of sage. Nia curled up on a rug in the corner, watching everything with sharp, silent eyes. She fetched water, she swept the floor, and she watched Mara with a mixture of awe and fear.

In the evenings, Kael worked on the cradle. Nia sat cross-legged near him, watching the shavings curl off the oak.

"It's like a castle," she whispered on the second night, touching the thick rim of the cradle.

Kael smiled, sanding the wood. "A fortress," he corrected. "To keep the world out."

"Strong," Elara declared from the table, where she was grinding herbs. "The heartbeat sounds like a war drum. Boom. Boom. Boom."

"A strong heart for the fields," Kael said firmly.

Elara chuckled. "You cannot choose who they will be, wood-worker. You can only build the boat. You cannot command the river. Nia, check the water. Is it boiling?"

"Yes, Mistress."

On the fourth afternoon, the waiting ended.

Kael was by the stream, cleaning trout. Nia was beside him,

holding the bucket. She was staring at the fish guts not with disgust, but with fascination at the abundance of life.

Suddenly, the fish in the pool upstream stopped swimming. They sank to the bottom, hovering in the shadows like stones.

The birds in the orchard cut off their song mid-chirp.

Nia looked around, shivering. "Why is it so quiet?" she whispered.

Kael stood up, the wet knife in his hand. He looked at the sky. Above the northern ridge, a wall of bruised, purple clouds was marching over the peaks. The air pressure dropped so fast his ears popped.

"Kael!"

The scream from the cabin was a command.

He dropped the fish. "Run, Nia," he told the girl. "Get to the house."

He looked at the darkening window where the first unnatural flash of lightning flickered in the distance. He realized then that Elara was right. He had built a cradle for a mouse, but the storm coming over the mountain—and the child coming with it—did not belong to small places.

Chapter 2: The War in the Skies

The cabin shuddered under the storm's assault. Its timber joints groaned as if the mountain itself were trying to crush it.

The clouds had settled directly over the valley, pinning them down with a weight that made the air thick and hard to breathe. Rain didn't fall; it was driven horizontally against the logs, sounding like handfuls of gravel thrown by an angry giant.

Inside, the air was hot and smelled of sweat and burning wood. Kael was vibrating with useless energy. He paced the small length of the floorboards, wringing a rag in his hands until his knuckles turned white. He checked the window and the door bolt. Then he loomed over the bed, his large shadow falling across Mara's sweat-slicked face.

"He's taking too long," Kael muttered, his voice tight with panic. "Why is he struggling so much?"

Elara didn't look up. She was arranging clean linens on a low stool, her movements precise and unhurried. Without turning, she snapped, "You are blocking the light, woodworker. Move."

Kael stumbled back as if she'd shoved him. "But the storm, Elara. Listen to it. My son shouldn't be born into this chaos."

"He needs a father who is not a moth fluttering around a flame," Elara cut him off. She stood up, her small frame seeming to fill the room. She pointed a bony finger at the corner. "Nia, get him a job before I hit him with a ladle."

Nia, who was crouching by the hearth feeding the fire, looked up with wide, terrified eyes. She scrambled to her feet, shoving a stack of towels into Kael's chest.

"Hold these, Master Kael," the girl squeaked. "Please. Just... hold them."

Kael retreated to the corner, clutching the towels like a shield. "I just want him to be strong," he whispered to the room, his eyes darting to the ceiling as the thunder roared again. "A strong boy to help rebuild the orchard after this."

CRACK.

A bolt of lightning struck somewhere in the apple orchard. The cabin shook violently, dust sifting down from the rafters. The thunder that followed was immediate and physical — a punch to the chest.

Mara cried out, the sound tearing from her throat.

Elara leaned over her, wiping the younger woman's forehead with a damp cloth. "Listen to me, girl," she murmured, her voice dropping under the roar of the wind. "Ignore the fool in the corner. Ignore the sky. The battle is in here."

"It hurts," Mara gasped, tears mixing with the sweat. "Elara, it feels like... like iron."

"Good," Elara said grimly. "Iron endures."

The next hour was a blur of noise and terror. The storm intensified, the lightning coming so fast that the gaps between the flashes disappeared. The room stuttered in a strobe-light horror of white brilliance and deep shadow.

Nia was huddled by the fire, her arms wrapped around her knees. She had seen storms in Oakhaven, but they were gray and miserable. This was different. This felt personal. It felt as if the sky was trying to hammer this specific cabin into the earth.

"Push, Mara! Now!" Elara barked.

Mara screamed, a raw, primal sound that competed with the wind.

Simultaneously, the sky ripped open. A sound unlike any thunder Kael had ever heard—a tearing, screeching crash—shook the floorboards so hard the water bucket tipped over, hissing into the fire.

And then, silence.

The thunder rolled away instantly, leaving a ringing void in the room.

In that sudden quiet, a new sound rose. Not the wail of a frightened infant, but a sharp, clear cry. A declaration.

Kael dropped the towels. He rushed forward, falling to his knees beside the bed. He was weeping, his fear breaking into exhaustion. "Is he here?" he choked out, looking at the bundle in Elara's arms. "Is he strong, Elara?"

Elara was silent. She wasn't looking at Kael. She was looking down at the child, her expression unreadable in the dim light of the dying fire.

Nia crept forward, peering over Elara's shoulder. The girl gasped. "Mistress... look."

Elara wrapped the linen tight. "Stronger than you know," she whispered.

"Let me see him," Kael demanded, reaching out with trembling hands. "Let me see the boy who weathered the storm."

Elara looked at him then. Her eyes were sharp, old, and filled with a pity that chilled Kael to the bone. She didn't correct him. She simply passed the bundle over.

"Look," she said.

Kael took the child. He looked down, expecting to see the dark fuzz of his own hair, or the fair wisps of Mara's.

At that moment, the storm fired its parting shot. A jagged bolt of lightning, blindingly bright, struck the ridge directly outside the window. The cabin was flooded with cold, electric white light.

For a heartbeat, the child was illuminated in stark relief.

Kael froze. Nia covered her mouth with her hand.

The baby was small, fierce, and alive. But it was her head that caught the fire of the lightning. The hair wasn't black. It wasn't blonde.

It shimmered with a metallic sheen. It flared in the sudden light like a coin dug up from the earth. Deep, oxidized copper. Verdigris.

Aerugo—the hue copper takes after it has endured the weather and remained.

The light faded, plunging them back into the gloom. Kael stared at the child, his mind reeling. He looked at the anatomy, realizing his mistake, realizing what Elara had known all along.

"A girl," Kael whispered, the word feeling foreign in his mouth.

Elara was wiping her hands on a rag, watching him closely. "You wanted a son to plow the fields, Kael," she said, her voice dry as dust.

Kael looked from the strange, copper fire on his daughter's head to the window where the storm was finally retreating. He felt a weight settle in his stomach—not of disappointment, but of fear. He had asked for a helper. The storm had sent him something else entirely.

"I wanted a son," Kael murmured, touching the baby's cheek with a calloused finger. "I wanted someone who could survive the world."

"Well," Elara said, packing her iron tools back into her bag with an ominous clatter. She looked at Nia, who was staring at the baby with wide, worshipful eyes. "You had best teach her quickly, wood-worker. Because looking at that sky... I don't think the world intends to let her survive."

Chapter 3: The Silent Sapling

The seasons in the valley did not march; they drifted.

The storm that had heralded Annajewel's arrival left scars. It had split the oldest apple tree down the middle, leaving a blackened, jagged stump that pointed at the sky like an accusatory finger. But the valley was resilient. By the time the child was walking, moss had covered the wound, and new saplings were pushing up through the black earth.

Life returned to its rhythm, but the silence had changed. Before, the silence of the valley had been empty. Now, it felt watched.

Old men from the hills would later say the birds changed first.

They would argue about it in low voices, years after they had stopped coming to the valley at all. The wrens no longer scattered at the snap of a twig. The crows lingered longer in the trees, tilting their heads as if listening for instruction rather than danger. Even the insects seemed to hum with purpose, their droning less frantic, more measured.

At first, Kael dismissed it as imagination. A man who spends too long alone begins to assign intention to weather and stone. But there were moments—small, quiet moments—that gnawed at him.

Seeds planted by careless toss took root where the soil should have been poor. Vines crept back from where he had cut them, not choking paths but framing them, as if marking where feet should go. When storms came, they bent around the orchard more often than they struck it. When frost settled, it spared the youngest shoots with a precision that felt deliberate.

The valley did not become gentler. It became attentive.

And Kael, who had survived by reading signs, could not tell whether the land was sheltering his child—or being taught by her.

Annajewel was not a loud child. She did not wail for milk in the night. She did not screech when she scraped her knees on the river stones. She simply... existed. She moved through the high grass with a stillness that unsettled Kael. He would look up from his hoeing to find her standing at the edge of the furrow, staring at him with those dark, serious eyes, her copper hair catching the sun like a beacon.

"She listens too much," Kael whispered to Mara one night. "Children should babble. They should chase butterflies. She watches the hawks."

"She is content," Mara said. But Kael saw the way Mara's hand trembled slightly. They both knew it wasn't contentment. It was patience.

There were nights when Mara woke to find Annajewel standing beside their bed.

She never cried. She never tugged at blankets or whispered for comfort. She would simply stand there, small hands folded, eyes reflecting the fire's dying embers. Mara would startle, heart hammering, before recognizing her own child.

"Anna," she would murmur, reaching out.

Annajewel would blink, as if returning from somewhere far away, then allow herself to be guided back to her pallet. She never explained why she rose. She never said she was frightened. When asked, she would only shrug and say, "The night was loud."

But Kael knew the night was not loud. The valley slept deeply. Too deeply.

Sometimes Annajewel sat for hours by the stream, dropping pebbles into the water, not to watch the ripples, but to listen to the sound they made when they vanished. Other children cried when they fell. Annajewel studied the bruise and waited for it to fade, as if pain were merely another season passing through her.

"She doesn't reach for us," Kael said once, voice low. "She doesn't need us the way children should."

Mara answered without looking up from her mending. "No," she said. "She lets us stay."

That was worse.

By her fourth winter, Kael began teaching her the rules of hiding.

The morning air on the southern ridge tasted of wet iron and old pine needles. It was a gray, biting cold that found the gaps in wool tunics and settled against the skin.

Kael adjusted his heavy leather gauntlets. They were stained black with years of sap and soil, stiff as cured wood. He looked down at Annajewel. She was four years old, a small figure wrapped in a brown cloak that was slightly too large, her breath puffing out in white clouds that vanished instantly in the wind.

"Do you remember the rule, Anna?" Kael asked. He kept his voice low, a habit he couldn't break even when they were alone.

Annajewel looked up at him. Her eyes were dark and serious, unblinking against the chill wind. "Stay small," she recited, her voice devoid of the sing-song quality other children had. "Stay small, and the hawk won't see the mouse."

"Good," Kael nodded. He gestured to the wall of vegetation before them.

To a stranger's eye, the southern ridge was a choked, impassable ravine. It was a chaotic tangle of blackberry vines, thick as ropes, armed with thorns the size of a cat's claw. Deadfall oak branches were woven through the living briars, creating a barrier that looked like the aftermath of a winter storm rather than the work of human hands.

This was Kael's masterpiece. He didn't build fences; fences implied something worth stealing lay behind them. He tended the brambles. He cultivated neglect.

"We are going through the gate," Kael whispered. "Watch me. Watch how I move."

He stepped up to the wall of thorns. He didn't push. Pushing invited resistance. He turned his body sideways, sucking in his breath to make himself a sliver of a man. He found the natural gap in the weave—a small, crooked tunnel near the ground where the deer sometimes passed.

Kael moved with the practiced tension of a man who expects pain. He lifted a heavy vine with his gauntleted hand, freezing as the thorns scraped against the leather with a sound like dry bones rattling. He stepped through, ducking low under a dead branch.

Halfway through, he twisted his hips to clear a particularly vicious knot of briars.

Snag.

The sound was sharp—wool tearing. A recurved thorn had hooked the shoulder of his tunic.

Kael froze. He cursed softly, a sharp hiss of frustration. He couldn't yank it free; the thorn would bury itself deeper. He had to stop, twist his arm back, and carefully unhook the fabric with his gloved fingers. The dry branches rattled around him, amplifying his struggle.

It took him a moment, his heart hammering a rhythm of annoyance. Clumsy, he thought. Old and clumsy.

He finally freed himself and stepped out onto the clear moss of the ridge side. He turned back, rubbing his shoulder.

"See?" he breathed, trying to hide his irritation. "The world catches you if you are not careful. It wants to hold you. You have to be smoother than the wood. Now, you try."

Annajewel stood on the other side of the bramble wall. She looked at the twisted tunnel of thorns. She looked at the dead branch that had forced her father to crouch.

She didn't turn sideways. She didn't suck in her breath .

"Anna," Kael warned, stepping forward instinctively. "Turn your shoulder. Make yourself thin."

Annajewel didn't answer. She simply walked forward.

18

Kael flinched. He braced himself for the sound of tearing cloth or the sharp cry of a child pricked by a needle-sharp point.

Neither came.

She moved into the tangle not as an intruder, but as if she were a draft of wind. She didn't fight the brush; she moved with it. When she reached the low-hanging dead branch, she didn't duck in a way that broke her stride. She simply tilted her head, just enough, adjusting her center of gravity so that the wood brushed the hood of her cloak without catching .

It was unnerving to watch. Kael had spent ten years learning the geometry of this thicket, memorizing which vines were loose and which were anchored. Annajewel treated it like water flowing through a sieve.

She stepped where the moss dampened the sound. She didn't disturb the dried leaves. The thorns that had snatched at Kael seemed to slide harmlessly off her wool cloak, finding no purchase.

She emerged on the ridge side three seconds faster than he had. Her breathing was even. Her cloak was untouched.

She looked up at him, then at the tear in his shoulder.

"You fought it, Papa," she said quietly.

Kael blinked, startled by the critique. "I was being careful. It's a dangerous path."

"It is only wood," she said, reaching out to touch a thorn on the vine nearest her. She didn't avoid the point; she pressed her finger against the flat of the thorn, acknowledging its sharpness without fearing it. "The wood is not your enemy. It is just wood."

Kael stared at her. The wind blew a strand of copper hair across her face, gleaming like a new coin against the gray sky.

"The world is full of enemies, Anna," Kael said, his voice harder than he intended. He felt a sudden, defensive need to make her understand the danger. "Thorns tear. Men take. Cold kills. You have to hide from them."

"If you hide," Annajewel said, dropping her hand, "you tell them you are prey."

She turned and looked down the slope, toward the trade road that snaked along the valley floor—the road where armies marched and refugees starved.

"I am not a mouse, Papa," she whispered.

Kael felt a chill that had nothing to do with the winter air. He reached out and adjusted her hood, pulling it forward to hide the metallic glint of her hair.

"For now," Kael said, his voice thick with a fear he couldn't name. "For now, you are a mouse. Because I cannot fight hawks."

Annajewel looked at him, her eyes old and measuring. She didn't argue. She simply took his hand. Her grip was warm, solid, and terrifyingly calm.

"Then I will be a mouse," she agreed. "Until the hawk lands."

After the brambles, Kael tried other lessons.

He taught her the sound of men walking carelessly: the scrape of a boot heel, the clink of iron rings. He showed her how smoke lies when it comes from a cookfire and how it tells the truth when it comes from a torch. He taught her the difference between a snapped branch and a broken one.

She learned all of it.

Too easily.

Where Kael learned through caution, Annajewel learned through alignment. She did not memorize dangers; she sensed imbalance. She could not tell him how she knew a path was unsafe—only that it felt crooked. When Kael ignored her, nothing happened at first. Then something small would go wrong. A tool would break. A snare would fail. A step would slide.

Kael began to listen to her the way sailors listen to the wind. Not with trust—never with trust—but with attention.

It unsettled him that she did not confuse hiding with fear.

When he told her to be quiet, she did not hold her breath. She breathed more deeply. When he warned her about men, she did not tense. She watched.

"You don't know what they do," Kael said once, sharper than he meant.

Annajewel tilted her head. "I know what they break."

As Annajewel grew, Kael's lessons grew to challenge her.

It was dusk, the time of day when the light turns blue and the shadows stretch long across the grass. Kael and Annajewel were checking the perimeter of the orchard.

Kael stopped dead. His hand shot out, not to his knife, but to his side, instinctively putting his body between Annajewel and the treeline.

"Still," he commanded in a whisper.

A doe stepped out of the shadows, her ears swiveling like radar dishes. A moment later, a fawn, its coat still dappled with white spots, stumbled out behind her. They were close—less than twenty paces.

The doe froze. She saw Kael. Her nostrils flared, scenting the man, the sweat, the danger. She stomped a front hoof—a warning. She perceived the threat.

Kael held his breath, making himself large, waiting for them to bolt. He knew the way of things: Man is the intruder; Beast is the survivor. They run, or they fight.

The doe made her move. She trotted sharply to the left, away from the fawn, making a noise in her throat. She was offering herself as a target, trying to draw the predator's eyes away from her offspring.

"Stay behind me," Kael murmured, tracking the mother, turning his body to shield his daughter.

But Annajewel didn't stay. She slipped quietly around his leg, stepping out from his shadow. She didn't move toward the deer;

she simply sat down in the tall grass, crossing her legs. She picked up a fallen apple blossom and began to twirl it.

The doe halted her decoy run. She looked back, confused. The large man was tracking her, but the small figure had disengaged.

The fawn had not followed its mother. Instead, the small creature took a tentative step toward Annajewel. It didn't look frightened. It looked... settled. To the fawn, the large man was a jagged rock of tension, but the girl in the grass felt like the earth itself— safe, grounded, and neutral.

"Anna," Kael hissed, terrified the mother would charge to protect the baby.

But the mother didn't charge. She watched her fawn walk within five feet of the girl. The fawn sniffed the air, acting as if the girl's presence offered more protection than the open woods.

It lowered its head to graze on a patch of clover near Annajewel's knee.

Annajewel didn't reach out. She didn't try to pet it. She ignored it completely, giving it the dignity of its own space.

For a long minute, the three of them stood in a tableau that broke every rule Kael knew. The predator, the prey, and the girl who was neither.

Eventually, the doe blew a soft breath through her nose. She walked back, nudged the fawn, and the two of them melted back into the woods.

Kael let out a breath he felt he'd been holding for years. "That... that isn't right," he muttered, wiping sweat from his palms. "They should have run."

Annajewel stood up, brushing grass from her skirt. "They run from fear, Papa. You were loud with fear. I was just sitting."

By her seventh year, Annajewel had become the steward of the valley.

It was midsummer, and the trout were running in the stream.

Kael stood knee-deep in the icy water, his spear poised. He was efficient, a provider who knew that winter was always coming.

A shadow passed over the gravel bed—a massive trout, nearly the length of his forearm, swimming sluggishly against the current. Its belly was swollen and pale.

Kael's eyes lit up. A fish that size meant oil, meant meat for days. He tensed, his arm cocking back for the strike.

"No."

The word was spoken softly from the bank, but it stopped Kael's arm as surely as if she'd grabbed it.

He looked up. Annajewel was sitting on a rock, her bare feet dangling in the water. She wasn't looking at him; she was looking at the fish.

"It's a prize, Anna," Kael argued, keeping his voice low so as not to spook the catch. "Look at the size of it."

"She is full of eggs," Annajewel said. "She is heavy with tomorrow."

Kael hesitated. "We need the meat. The smokehouse is getting low."

Annajewel looked at him then. "If you take her, you take the hundred fish she will make. You take the food from the heron. You take the life from the river." She pointed to a smaller, leaner fish darting in the shallows. "Take the bachelor. He has lived his life. She is still carrying hers."

Kael looked at the massive fish, an easy target. He looked at the smaller, quicker one. He felt a flash of irritation—the pragmatism of survival warring with something deeper.

He lowered the spear. He let the mother pass.

Ten minutes later, he speared the smaller male.

As he waded ashore, Nia arrived.

The apprentice midwife was twenty now, her face gaunt, her clothes hanging loose on her frame. She came down the path carrying a basket of empty jars to trade. She stopped, watching Kael gut the small fish while the massive female swam safely upstream.

"You let the big one go," Nia said, her voice raspy with a hunger she tried to hide. "I saw it from the ridge. You could have fed a family for a week with that beast."

Kael looked at Annajewel, who was gathering mint leaves by the water's edge. "We are not eating for a week, Nia," he said, repeating the lesson he had just learned. "We are eating for next year."

Nia sat heavily on the grass. "Next year," she whispered, looking at the lush green of the valley with a mixture of envy and despair. "In Oakhaven, we don't think about next year. We just try to survive tonight."

Annajewel walked over and placed a bundle of fresh mint in Nia's lap. "Then take this," the child said. "For the tea. It calms the stomach when there is no bread."

Nia looked at the mint, then at the girl whose hair burned like copper in the sun. "You live in a dream down here, little one," Nia said, her voice trembling. "But dreams wake up."

That night, Kael walked the ridge alone.

The wind was high, bending the grasses flat, and he imagined his daughter standing there years from now, hair blazing, unbowed. The thought did not comfort him. Trees that grow straight and tall draw lightning.

Below him, the valley lay calm. The stream sang. The orchard breathed.

He understood then that Annajewel did not belong to the valley in the way he had hoped. She was not its secret. She was its declaration.

The land did not hide her.

It was preparing her.

And Kael, who had spent his life teaching his family to disappear, realized that no lesson he knew could teach his daughter how to survive a world that would not look away.

Kael cleaned his knife, watching the water run red. He had taught her to listen. He had not taught her to be afraid. He had taught his daughter to respect the land, but he hadn't taught her to fear the men who would burn it. And as he looked at her standing fearlessly by the apprentice, he realized the time for hiding was ending. The sapling was growing tall, and tall trees on the ridge cannot hide from the wind.

Chapter 4: The Sticks and Stones

The world beyond the ridge was not green. It was the color of old bruises.

The road that led down from the ridge bore the marks of that bruising. Wagon ruts had hardened into crooked scars, filled with stagnant water the color of old tea. Broken fence posts leaned at angles that suggested they had not fallen by accident. Here and there, scraps of cloth fluttered from thorns—mute evidence of hurried passage and hands that had not been gentle.

Annajewel felt the change before Kael said a word. The air itself seemed thinner, sharper, as if it carried edges. In the valley, sound settled. Here, it skittered. Voices echoed where they should not have, and even the birds seemed to call only once before going silent again.

Kael adjusted the strap of his pack and slowed his pace, his eyes scanning the road ahead, then the slopes to either side. This was not land that welcomed lingering. It endured it.

Annajewel tightened her grip on his hand, not in fear, but in acknowledgment. Whatever rules governed the valley did not extend beyond the ridge.

For eight years, Kael had kept the world at bay. He had woven the brambles tighter, hidden the path with fallen logs, and taught his daughter to be a ghost in her own home. But salt could not be grown in an orchard, and iron could not be harvested from a river.

The trip to Oakhaven was inevitable.

"Keep the hood up," Kael warned, kneeling in the dirt to adjust the heavy woolen cloak Annajewel wore. He pulled the fabric forward until her face was a shadow and the copper fire of her hair was completely extinguished. "And keep your eyes down.

You are a mouse today, Anna. Mice do not look at hawks."

Annajewel stood still, letting him fuss. She was tall for eight, with limbs that were strong from climbing the ancient apple trees. Under the hood, her eyes were not the fearful eyes of a mouse. They were measuring.

"I understand, Papa," she said, her voice calm.

Kael hesitated. He checked the knife at his belt, hoisted the sack of dried apple rings over his shoulder, and took her hand.

"Stay close," he muttered. "And say nothing."

Oakhaven was a shock to the senses.

As they descended the trade road, the smell hit them first—a thick, cloying soup of unwashed bodies, woodsmoke, and open sewage. Annajewel wrinkled her nose, but she didn't complain. She watched.

The town was crowded for market day, but it wasn't a happy crowd. It was a desperate shuffle of gray figures. Men with hollow cheeks haggled over turnips that were mostly rot. Women clutched shawls tight around thin shoulders, eyeing the mercenary patrols that swaggered through the mud.

Annajewel saw the soldiers. They wore rusted chainmail and cloaks dyed a dirty crimson. They laughed too loud. They took apples from carts without paying.

To Annajewel, who knew only the abundance of the valley where trees gave fruit freely and fish offered themselves to the spear, this place made no sense.

She tried to understand it the way she understood the river.

In the valley, hunger was a message, not a verdict. It told you when to move, when to wait, when to take less so that more would come later. Here, hunger clung to people like a sickness. It bent backs and sharpened voices. It turned neighbors into competitors and children into liabilities.

Annajewel watched a woman argue over a basket of onions so

small it would not have fed Kael for a day. She saw a man hide a heel of bread inside his coat and flinch when no one had even looked his way. She saw guards laugh as a merchant bowed and scraped, thanking them for what they had already taken.

Nothing here was shared. Nothing here was allowed to rest.

The valley taught that balance sustained life. Oakhaven taught that taking was survival. Annajewel could not reconcile the two. She only knew that one of them was lying. It was a place of Taking.

Kael moved with his head down, gripping her hand so tight it hurt. He found a merchant he knew, a man named Tobin who traded iron nails for dried fruit.

"Kael," Tobin grunted, eyeing the sack. "You made the trip. The roads are bad. The Iron Army is moving south, they say."

"The roads are always bad," Kael replied, keeping his voice low, ignoring the news of war. He set the sack on the cart. "I need nails. And salt."

While the men haggled, Kael's grip on Annajewel's hand loosened slightly. He was focused on the trade, counting the nails to ensure he wasn't cheated.

Annajewel stepped back. She didn't wander far, just to the edge of the cart, near the alleyway that ran behind the blacksmith's shop.

There were sounds coming from the alley. Not the sounds of trade. Oakhaven had many kinds of noise, and Annajewel had already begun to sort them.

There was the sound of bargaining, sharp and repetitive, like stones struck together until one cracked. There was the sound of hunger, softer but constant, carried in the wet coughs and hurried footsteps of those who did not wish to be noticed. And then there was this—impact without rhythm, breath forced out of lungs, pain passed from hand to body to ground.

It was the sound Kael never allowed in the valley. The sound of strength proving itself by choosing something weaker.

Annajewel paused at the mouth of the alley, listening.

She did not look back to see if her father was watching. Whatever was happening here had already stepped outside the rules she knew, and rules, once broken, demanded correction.

She moved forward, into the dark towards the sounds of wet thuds and stifled whimpers.

Leaning against the wall of the smithy, hidden in the shadows, was a boy. He was perhaps sixteen, wearing the ill-fitting leather armor of a mercenary recruit. He had a bored, cruel face, and he was watching something further down the alley with mild amusement.

Annajewel ignored the recruit. She stepped past him, into the gloom.

Three boys, roughly twelve years old, stood in a circle. They were ragged and dirty, passing the pain of their lives down to someone smaller. In the center of the circle huddled a child—a ball of rags and grime, curling on the mud to protect his head.

"Where is it?" the tallest bully sneered, kicking the child in the ribs. "The baker said you stole a crust. Cough it up, rat."

The child on the ground sobbed. "I ate it. I was hungry."

"Hungry?" The second bully picked up a handful of mud. "Eat this, then." He shoved the mud into the child's face.

Annajewel watched. In the valley, the strong protected the weak. The apple tree shaded the sapling. The doe distracted the wolf from the fawn.

This was wrong. It was a violation of the natural law.

"Stop."

The word was quiet, but it echoed in the narrow stone alley.

The bullies turned. The teenage mercenary recruit by the wall straightened up, his interest piqued.

"Get lost, mouse," the tall bully spat. "Unless you want a kicking too."

Annajewel didn't leave. She looked around the alley. It was

littered with debris. She reached down and picked up a piece of ash wood, likely a broken tool handle. It was heavy, smooth, and solid.

"He is too small," Annajewel said. She stepped forward. She didn't hold the stick like a toy. She held it balanced, her weight centered.

The bullies laughed. "Look at this," the tall one said, grinning. "A hero." He lunged.

Annajewel didn't flinch. She stepped into the attack.

She swung the ash stick. It wasn't a wild, flailing swing. It was a short, sharp crack.

The wood connected with the bully's shin. He howled, hitting the mud instantly.

The teenage recruit by the wall let out a low whistle of appreciation.

The other two bullies rushed her. Annajewel dropped the stick and ducked under a clumsy swing. She grabbed a handful of loose gravel from the ground and flung it upward—not at the body, but at the eyes.

The second boy screamed, clawing at his face, blinded.

The third boy hesitated. He looked at the girl, then at the mercenary recruit watching them.

"Don't look at me," the recruit drawled, crossing his arms. "She's beating you fair and square."

The third boy ran.

Annajewel knelt beside the child on the ground. She reached into her pocket and pulled out a dried apple ring—sweet, chewy, and golden. "Eat," she said.

"Anna!"

Kael appeared at the mouth of the alley, his face pale as milk. He saw the violence, the fallen boys, and the mercenary recruit watching his daughter.

He rushed forward, grabbing her arm. "We are leaving. Now."

He dragged her toward the street. But as she turned, the tall bully on the ground lashed out in a final act of spite. He grabbed the hem of her cloak and yanked.

The clasp snapped. The hood fell back.

For a second, the gloom of the alley was pierced by color. Her hair tumbled free—deep copper, dulled and darkened as if it had endured weather and time. In the gray, mud-stained world of Oakhaven, it did not belong.

The mercenary recruit pushed himself off the wall. His bored expression vanished. He stared at the hair, then at the girl's face. He looked like he was seeing a ghost.

"What are you?" the recruit whispered.

Kael shoved the bully back, pulling the hood up with frantic hands. He scooped Annajewel into his arms, hiding her face against his shoulder. He ran.

He ran through the market, ignoring Tobin calling after him. He ran past the guards, past the misery. He didn't stop until they were a mile up the trade road, lungs burning.

He set her down on a flat rock, his hands shaking.

"You cannot do that," Kael choked out. "You cannot fight the world, Anna. There are too many of them."

Annajewel looked back toward the town. "There are many of them," she agreed, her voice raspy and old. "But they are cowards, Papa. They only fight the small."

Kael looked at his daughter—eight years old, with the heart of a Titan. He realized then that his fortress of brambles had failed. He hadn't protected her from the world. He had simply delayed the war.

Back in the alley, the teenage recruit was still standing there. He looked at the stick on the ground. He looked at the spot where the copper-haired girl had stood.

"Torian!" a sergeant bellowed from the street.

"Quit loitering, boy! We march in the morning."

Torian turned, picking up his spear. He looked back at the alley one last time. He touched his own bruised knuckles, remembering the girl's quiet, efficient violence.

"A mouse," Torian muttered to himself, a strange smile touching his lips. "That was no mouse."

Interlude I: The Wolf's Den

The tavern in Oakhaven didn't have a name, just a sign above the door depicting a cracked tankard. It was the kind of place that survived not because it was liked, but because it was necessary. Men came here to forget where they slept and why. The floorboards were warped from years of spilled drink and heavy boots, and the walls bore old knife marks that no one bothered to repair, trophies of arguments long settled or long buried.

Voices pressed in from every side, loud enough to drown out thought but never quite loud enough to smother it. Laughter flared and died without joy. Dice clattered on tabletops scarred with burn rings and bloodstains, the sound sharp and final, like bones striking stone.

This was where Oakhaven bled off its excess anger, where men who had nowhere else to put their violence let it drip onto wood and straw instead of the street. No one expected mercy here. No one came looking for justice.

Torian had learned that quickly.

It smelled of sour ale, wet dog, and aggressive men.

Torian sat in the corner, nursing a cup of watered-down wine. At sixteen, he was the youngest recruit in the Red Cloaks, a mercenary company that had seen better days. His armor was secondhand leather, stiff with old sweat, and his spear had a wobble in the shaft.

"Drink up, boy!" Sergeant Kroll slammed a heavy hand on Torian's shoulder, nearly knocking him off the bench. Kroll was a mountain of scarred meat, his beard matted with crumbs. "We march at dawn. You can't kill Northern savages on an empty stomach."

Torian straightened up, forcing a grin he didn't feel. "Where are we heading, Sergeant? The rumors say the Iron Empire has crossed the White River."

The table went quiet. The other mercenaries—men with missing teeth and eyes like flint—exchanged dark looks.

"The Iron Empire," Kroll spat on the floor. "They aren't an empire. They're a machine. They don't fight for gold, and they don't fight for land. They fight because some Emperor in the north thinks the world needs to be hammered flat."

"Fifty thousand of them," a one-eyed crossbowman muttered into his ale. "Wearing plate armor so shiny you can see your own death in it."

"And that's why we're going south," Kroll laughed, though it sounded forced. "Let the lords fight the Iron men. We're paid to guard the grain caravans heading to the coast. Easy coin. Easy killing."

Torian looked down at his hands. His knuckles were still bruised from a tavern brawl two nights ago. He was good at fighting. He was quick, mean, and didn't mind the sight of blood. That's why Kroll had recruited him from the gutter.

But his mind kept drifting back to the alleyway behind the smithy.

He had seen cruelty before. Oakhaven was full of it, handed down like an inheritance. Strong hands took from weaker ones, and the town called it order. The Red Cloaks were built on the same bargain. You learned quickly who could be struck and who could not, who mattered and who existed only to be used.

The girl had not followed that logic.

She had not postured or threatened. She had not looked to the watching recruit for approval or permission. She had simply stepped forward and ended what should not have been happening. Not with rage, not with pleasure, but with a precision that left no room for argument.

Torian tried to tell himself it was nothing. A fluke. A clever child with a stick and good luck. But the memory refused to dull. It lodged in him like grit under the skin, irritating, inescapable.

Violence, as Torian understood it, was a transaction. Pain for obedience. Fear for control.

What he had witnessed in the alley was something else entirely.

He thought of the girl in the brown cloak. She couldn't have been more than eight years old. A mouse.

But mice didn't move like that.

Torian had seen veterans fight. They fought with anger. They grunted, they sweated, they swung wild haymakers meant to crush bone. It was messy work.

The girl hadn't been angry. She had been... absolute.

Crack. Shin. Woosh. Gravel. Stop.

It was the most efficient violence Torian had ever seen. It didn't look like brawling; it looked like cleaning.

"What are you brooding on, pup?" Kroll asked, leaning in, his breath smelling of onions. "Scared of the march?"

Torian looked up. "I saw something today. In the market."

"A whore?" Kroll leered. "A thief?"

"A girl," Torian said quietly. "She took down three of the baker's boys. She didn't use a knife. She just... dismantled them."

The table erupted in laughter.

"Listen to him!" the crossbowman jeered. "Torian the Terror, impressed by a schoolyard scrap."

"It wasn't a scrap," Torian insisted, though he didn't know why he was defending her. "She moved like she knew what they were going to do before they did it. And her hair..." He trailed off. He remembered that flash of copper. It hadn't looked like hair. It had looked like a helmet catching the sun.

"Hair?" Kroll slapped him on the back again, harder this time. "Forget the girls, Torian. You want to survive this life? You look at two things: the coin in your hand and the tip of your spear. Everything else is just a distraction."

Kroll stood up, raising his tankard. "To the Red Cloaks! May we die rich and drunk!"

"Rich and drunk!" the men roared back.

They leaned in the same way the boys had—eager, careless, certain no one would stop them.

Torian raised his cup, but he didn't drink. He looked out the grime-smeared window toward the dark ridges of the foothills. Somewhere up there, the girl with the copper hair was hiding.

He looked at his own spear leaning against the wall. It was a weapon of war, designed to kill men for money.

Then he thought of the girl's ash stick. A piece of broken garbage that she had turned into a tool of correction.

They fight because they are hungry, she had said to the sobbing child. We fight because we are paid.

Torian felt a sudden, cold knot in his stomach. He wondered if, for all their armor and their shouting, the men at this table were the weak ones. Scavengers, picking at whatever was left.

The girl in the alley was something else entirely.

"I'm going to sleep," Torian said abruptly, standing up.

"Dream of gold, boy!" Kroll shouted after him.

Torian walked out into the cold night air. The wind was blowing from the north, carrying the scent of snow and iron. The war was coming. The real war. And for the first time, Torian wondered if he was on the wrong side of it.

Chapter 5: The Titan

Two winters passed, and the world grew colder.

The news from the north was no longer a rumor; it was a vibration in the ground. The Iron Empire was chewing its way south, devouring duchies and kingdoms with mechanical indifference. Refugees began to trickle down the trade roads—broken families pushing carts piled with everything they owned, their eyes hollowed out by what they had seen.

Some did not make it as far as Oakhaven.

Kael saw the evidence when he walked the ridge at dawn: abandoned carts stripped of anything useful, wheel spokes snapped for firewood, a child's shoe lying alone in the mud where no child remained to claim it. Crows gathered early now, bold and unafraid, hopping close enough that he could see the dried blood on their beaks.

Those who reached the town carried more than their belongings. They carried the memory of roads where no one helped, of villages that shut their gates, of men in armor who counted lives the way merchants counted coin. The Iron Empire did not need to arrive to make itself known. Its shadow traveled ahead of it, teaching people how to abandon hope efficiently.

By the time the first families appeared at the foot of the ridge, the world beyond the valley had already decided what kind of war this would be.

Oakhaven, already a place of gray misery, became a purgatory. The local lords, terrified of the approaching Iron men, had levied a "War Tax." They stripped the granaries. They took the horses. They took the last of the copper coins.

But in the unnamed valley, the apple trees bloomed white and defiant.

The contrast gnawed at Kael.

He walked the orchard rows that morning with a sense of unease he could not shake. Blossoms fell at his feet like quiet snowfall, piling against his boots. Bees moved lazily from branch to branch, indifferent to the rumors that had set the wider world trembling. Everything here behaved as if the future were certain.

That certainty felt dangerous.

Kael pruned where pruning was needed, thinned where thinning would help the trees bear next year, and marked which branches would be cut for firewood when the season turned. He worked harder than necessary, as if labor itself could anchor the valley against what pressed in from beyond the ridge.

Yet even as his hands moved through familiar motions, his eyes kept lifting toward the road. The valley was flourishing at the very moment the world was failing, and Kael understood enough of fate to know that such imbalance never went unnoticed for long.

From the ridge, Kael watched the road. It was clogged with a fresh column of refugees. He tightened the bramble gate, adding more thorns, more deadwood.

"We stay small," he muttered, though the words felt like ash in his mouth.

He turned to walk back down into the valley, but stopped.

Coming up the path from the cabin was a figure.

Annajewel was ten years old now. She had grown tall, her limbs lengthening into the wiry strength of a sapling oak. She wore a simple tunic of rough wool, and her feet were bare, finding purchase on the slick rocks.

She carried two heavy baskets, one in each hand, filled with smoked trout and dried apples.

Kael recognized the baskets at once. They were the old ones, woven tight and reinforced at the handles with wire scavenged years ago from a broken trap. He had kept them for emergencies only. Each was heavy enough that he would normally have taken one and left the other behind.

Annajewel stood balanced beneath the weight, her shoulders squared, her stance sure. She had packed the food carefully—fish wrapped in cloth to keep the oil from seeping, apples layered so they would not bruise. This was not a child's impulsive theft from the smokehouse. It was a deliberate inventory.

Kael felt the sharp edge of something like betrayal, followed immediately by shame. She had not taken more than the valley could spare. She had calculated.

Looking at her then, Kael understood that she had already decided to go before he reached the ridge. The question was never whether she would leave the valley. It was whether he would walk with her.

"Where are you going?" Kael asked, blocking the path.

Annajewel didn't stop until she was two paces from him. She set the baskets down. She wasn't out of breath.

"To the bridge," she said. Her voice had lost its childish pitch; it was low, resonant.

"The bridge is five miles away," Kael said, his voice rising. "It is on the main road. Soldiers are there. Thieves are there."

"And children are there," Annajewel replied. "Nia told me. There are families sleeping under the stone arch. They have eaten nothing but boiled grass for three days."

"That is not our burden," Kael snapped, fear making him harsh. "We cannot feed the world, Anna. If we give this away, what happens when the winter comes for us?"

Annajewel looked at him. She didn't argue. She didn't plead. She simply picked up the baskets again. The muscles in her forearms corded with the effort, but her face remained serene.

"The winter is far, Papa. The hunger is here."

She stepped around him.

Kael reached out to grab her arm, to physically stop her as he had done when she was small. But his hand hovered in the air.

He looked at her back—straight, unyielding, carrying a burden a grown man would find heavy. There was a density to her presence now. She didn't feel like a child disobeying a parent. She felt like a force of nature moving downhill. To stop her would be like trying to hold back the tide with a spoon.

Kael dropped his hand. He cursed softly, checked his knife, and followed her.

The stone bridge over the White River was a choke point for the refugees. A makeshift camp had sprung up in its shadow—a collection of ragged tents and desperate people huddled around small, smoky fires.

When Annajewel walked into the camp, the noise died down. Not because she demanded it—because their bodies chose quiet before their minds could argue

She was striking. Even in her rough clothes, with her hood pulled up to hide the copper fire, she moved with a purpose that cut through the chaos. She didn't wander. She walked straight to the center of the camp, where a group of orphans sat in the mud.

Nia was there. The apprentice midwife looked skeletal now, her eyes sunk deep in her skull. She was trying to wash a feverish child's face with a dirty rag.

"Nia," Annajewel said.

Nia looked up. When she saw the baskets, she burst into tears.

"You came," Nia sobbed. "I told them... I told them the girl from the green valley would come."

Annajewel didn't waste time on greetings. "Organize them," she commanded. "The sick in the center, near the fire. The smallest ones first."

It wasn't a suggestion. It was spoken with a certainty that left no room for argument.

Nia, ten years older than the child, scrambled to obey. "Yes. Yes, of course."

For the next hour, Annajewel was a whirlwind. She didn't just hand out food; she managed the chaos. She broke the smoked fish into portions. She stopped a large man who tried to snatch an apple from a child's hand—not by hitting him, but by gripping his wrist and staring into his eyes until he backed away, ashamed.

Kael watched from the edge of the firelight, his hand on his knife, awestruck.

She was ten years old. But she moved among these desperate, broken people like a queen moving among her subjects. They didn't push. They didn't riot. They waited for her to speak.

"Titan," Kael whispered to himself, the word chilling him.

Then, trouble arrived.

A patrol of the local Lord's guards rode up to the bridge. They were collecting the "toll"—a euphemism for robbing refugees of whatever scraps they had left. The leader, a man with a greasy mustache and a tarnished breastplate, spotted the baskets.

"Well now," the guard sneered, dismounting. "Smoked trout? That's too fine for rats." He walked toward Annajewel, his hand resting on the hilt of his sword. "By order of the Lord Governor, all provisions are subject to the war tax."

The refugees cowered. Nia shrank back, clutching the feverish child.

Annajewel didn't move. She stood between the basket and the guard. She barely reached his chest.

"Move aside, girl," the guard barked.

"No," Annajewel said.

The camp went silent. The only sound was the rushing of the river.

The guard laughed, a nervous, angry sound. "No? Do you see

this steel, girl? I can take what I want."

"You can," Annajewel agreed. She looked up at him, her hood falling back slightly, revealing the copper glint at her temples. "You have a sword. You can cut me down. You can take the fish."

She took a step toward him.

"But you will not eat it," she said softly. "It will turn to ash in your mouth. You will remember the face of the child you starved, and you will never sleep without hearing his cry."

The guard hesitated. It was absurd. A peasant girl threatening him with... what? Guilt?

But looking into her eyes, he felt a sudden, crushing awareness. Not of her—but of himself, standing armed before the hungry.

He licked his lips. He looked at the refugees watching him. For the first time, he felt how many eyes there were. He looked at the strange, metallic hair of the child.

"Keep your stinking fish," the guard muttered, backing away. He swung onto his horse, looking rattled. "It's probably rotten anyway."

He spurred his horse and galloped away, his men following in confused silence.

Nia let out a shuddering breath. "How?" she whispered. "How did you do that?"

Annajewel turned back to the basket, picking up a dried apple. "He was afraid," she said simply. "Fear makes men weak. Purpose makes them strong."

She handed the apple to the feverish child.

Kael stepped out of the shadows. He looked at his daughter, then at the retreating soldiers. He realized that she wasn't just saving these people. She was building an army. Not of soldiers, but of believers.

It did not look like an army. There were no banners, no drilled ranks, no shouted commands. There were only people who had been seen when they expected to be ignored, fed when they expected to be forgotten.

Around the fire, shoulders straightened. Hands steadied. A woman who had been clutching her child as if bracing for a blow now sat upright, rocking slowly, humming something low and tuneless. A man who had arrived snarling and suspicious found himself holding a cup of broth and waiting his turn for more, uncertain how to behave in the absence of force.

Annajewel did not promise them victory. She did not speak of war or retribution. She gave them order where there had been panic, and purpose where there had been only endurance. That was enough.

Kael understood then that belief did not require speeches. It required a moment when fear was interrupted and replaced with something steadier. Once that happened, men would carry the memory with them far beyond the reach of any single fire.

"We need more wood for the fire," Annajewel said to him, as if she hadn't just stared down an armed man. "Papa, will you help?"

Kael looked at her. He nodded slowly. "Yes, Anna. I will help."

He went to gather wood, knowing that he was no longer the protector. He was the follower. The hiding that had saved him could no longer save her.

Interlude II: The Iron March

The mud on the Northern Road was a foot deep, churned into a freezing paste by fifty thousand pairs of boots.

The march had a rhythm, and it was not heroic. It was the sound of weight applied again and again until the ground gave up trying to resist. Iron rims ground against stone. Leather creaked. Breath came out in pale clouds and was trampled flat by the men behind it.

No songs carried down the column. Songs wasted air. Orders were passed hand to hand, brief and numerical, stripped of anything that might slow them. When a man slipped and fell, the pace did not change. Two others hauled him upright by his straps and pushed him forward until his feet remembered their purpose.

The Iron Empire did not advance like a storm. It advanced like a millstone—slow, deliberate, and impossible to argue with once it began to turn.

General Valerius did not ride a white stallion. He rode a heavy draft horse, bred for pulling plows, because a warhorse would have snapped a leg in this muck miles ago.

He pulled his fur collar tight against the sleet. He was a man of numbers, not speeches. He looked down the line of the column. It stretched back as far as he could see—a river of gray steel and wet leather winding through the burnt-out remains of a hamlet.

"Report," Valerius said, not turning his head.

His adjutant, a young captain with ink-stained fingers, rode up beside him. "The forward scouts have reached the White River, General. The bridge is intact."

"And the resistance?"

"Scattered, sir. The local lords have retreated to their keeps.

They are burning their own fields to deny us forage."

Valerius nodded. It was the logical move. It was also a waste of time. "They think we eat grain," he muttered. "We eat territory."

He looked at the village they were passing. It wasn't burning anymore; the fires had gone out days ago. Now it was just black skeletons of houses. There were no bodies—his rear guard was efficient at disposal to prevent disease. There was just silence and the smell of wet ash.

"The men are tired, General," the adjutant ventured. "The pace has been... aggressive."

Valerius looked at the soldier marching nearest to him. The man was covered in mud, his face a mask of exhaustion. He didn't look heroic. He looked like a laborer carrying a heavy load. But he kept walking. Step. Step. Step.

"Fatigue is a calculation," Valerius said flatly. "If we stop, the cold sets in. If we stop, the lords to the south have time to unite. We do not stop."

He reached into his saddlebag and pulled out a map. It was a grid of lines and elevations, devoid of art. His finger traced the route south, past the White River, toward the cluster of foothills that bordered the coast.

"What is this settlement?" Valerius asked, tapping a smudge of ink near the ridge line.

"Oakhaven, sir. A trade post. Negligible strategic value."

"Does it have walls?"

"A palisade, old and rotting."

"Does it have food?"

"Likely."

Valerius marked it with a piece of charcoal. "Then it has value."

He rolled the map. He didn't feel a thrill of conquest. He didn't feel hatred for the people of Oakhaven. He felt the same way a carpenter feels about a knot in the wood—it was just something to be planed down.

Valerius had learned long ago that sentiment was a kind of inefficiency. Men who hated their enemies wasted strength on anger. Men who feared them hesitated. He preferred neither. Wood did not deserve hatred, and it did not merit fear. It required pressure, applied correctly, until it changed shape.

That was why the Iron Empire endured. Not because its soldiers were braver or crueler than others, but because they were trained to think of conquest as labor. You did not rush a harvest. You cut when the grain bent the right way. You stacked what was useful and burned the rest.

He did not ask whether the people in the path of the march were good or bad. Those questions belonged to priests and poets. His concern was simpler: would the road hold, would the wagons roll, would the men keep moving.

And if something resisted?

Then it would be worn down, measured stroke by measured stroke, until resistance became material.

"General," the adjutant said, pointing ahead.

A group of prisoners was being herded off the road to make way for the supply wagons. They were local militia—ragged men with pitchforks and hunting bows who had tried to hold a river crossing. They looked terrified, shivering in the sleet, waiting for the order that would end them.

Valerius didn't look at their faces. He looked at their boots.

"Those men have good leather," Valerius noted. "Take the boots before you execute them. The Third Cohort is reporting rot."

"Yes, General."

Valerius kicked his draft horse forward. The beast grunted, pulling its hooves out of the sucking mud. The sound of the army was a low, grinding thrum—not a chant, not a war cry, just the heavy, industrial noise of iron moving south.

Valerius didn't fear the coming battle. He didn't fear the southern lords. He checked the sun's position through the gray clouds. They were three miles behind schedule. That was the only enemy that mattered.

Chapter 6: The Quinquennium

Five years of rain and sun turned the sapling into a tree.

The change had not been sudden. It came the way erosion comes—grain by grain, season by season, unnoticed until the shape of things was no longer the same. Each year left its mark: shoulders broadening under work, hands toughening under callus, eyes learning when to look away and when to hold.

Kael had marked the years by practical measures. How much firewood Annajewel could carry without slowing. How long she could work before hunger reached her. When she stopped asking permission and began stating intention. None of it frightened him at first. Growth was natural. Growth was expected.

What unsettled him was how little of it needed correction.

She did not rebel. She did not test limits. She absorbed them, adjusted them, and then quietly exceeded them. The valley shaped her, but she did not bend under its weight. She bore it.

By the time the sapling could no longer be hidden among smaller trees, Kael understood that the years had been preparing her for something he had no words for yet—and no way to stop.

Annajewel was fifteen. The awkward angles of childhood had smoothed out.

She moved through the camp without visible intention.

That was what unsettled people later, when they tried to explain it. She did not arrive with purpose or announcement. She did not seek anyone out. She simply crossed spaces that were already crowded, and those spaces loosened around her.

Men stepped aside without realizing they had done so. Conversations thinned, then trailed off, as if the words had reached a natural ending they hadn't noticed approaching. A woman arguing over a bowl of stew fell silent mid-sentence, staring past Annajewel's shoulder before shaking herself and resuming in a lower voice.

Annajewel did not look at them. She did not register the shifts. She walked as she always had—balanced, economical, her attention fixed on the work ahead.

Children noticed first.

They drifted closer, drawn by something they could not name. Not excitement. Not comfort. A sense of alignment, like standing in the right place during a strong wind.

One small boy followed her for half the length of the camp before realizing he had no idea why he was doing it and scurrying away, embarrassed.

Not everyone yielded.

A miner with a scarred cheek deliberately held his ground as she approached, jaw set, shoulders squared. Annajewel adjusted her path without breaking stride, passing him close enough that he could smell the mint and earth on her clothes. The man exhaled only after she was gone, irritated by the relief that followed.

By evening, no one would have been able to say where she had gone.

Only that the camp felt different when she wasn't there.

She was tall, with the broad shoulders of someone who hauled water and the calloused hands of someone who shaped wood. Her face, once round and soft, had sharpened.

In the privacy of the cabin, Mara watched her daughter braid her hair. The copper strands were heavy, thick as rope, falling to the small of her back.

"Tie it up, Anna," Mara said, her voice tight. "Under the cap."

Annajewel paused, her fingers weaving the plait. "The cap catches on the branches."

"Tie it up," Mara repeated. She looked at the mirror—a polished sheet of tin Kael had traded for. She saw what the world would see: the high cheekbones, the pale throat, the fire of the hair. It was a beacon. "It isn't safe."

Annajewel finished the braid. She coiled it tight against her skull and pulled the rough woolen cap down, hiding the color. She looked in the tin sheet. She checked for dirt. She checked for loose strands. She saw a mechanism for work.

Mara watched her from the doorway, hands clenched in the hem of her apron.

Once, she had braided that hair with songs, counting strands the way mothers do, turning the act into comfort. Now the motions were efficient, practiced, stripped of ritual. The girl in the reflection did not linger on her own face. She checked fastenings, tested balance, and moved on.

Mara felt the old instinct rise—the urge to soften, to delay, to insist on small vanities that marked safety. She swallowed it. Vanity had never protected anyone. The world beyond the ridge did not care how carefully a woman was raised.

Still, as Annajewel turned away from the mirror, Mara felt the weight of what was being surrendered. Not beauty—beauty endured whether it was hidden or not—but innocence. And once surrendered, that was not a thing that could be reclaimed.

She said nothing more. Words had already been spent.

"I am going to the bridge," Annajewel said, turning from the reflection. "Nia sent word. The fever is back in the camp."

"Take the high path," Mara said, looking at the floor.

"I always do."

The refugee camp at the bridge had become a permanent scar on the landscape.

The scar had learned to function.

What had once been a chaos of shouting and shoving had settled into patterns. Fires burned in predictable rings. Water was drawn in lines that no one remembered agreeing upon. Even disputes followed a rhythm—voices rising, stalling, then breaking apart before fists were thrown.

Annajewel had not organized any of it.

But when she walked through the camp, people found themselves waiting.

A man with a cart of turnips paused mid-argument, hands still raised, eyes tracking her path until she passed out of sight. Two women haggling over bandages stopped, exchanged a look, and quietly split the bundle without further complaint. A child crying near the riverbank fell silent when Annajewel knelt nearby, though she never touched him.

By dusk, people had begun to time things around her without knowing they were doing so.

Food was distributed when she was present. Fires were lit after she passed. Work seemed to steady when she was nearby and fray when she left. No one said it aloud, but the camp had begun to lean.

Nia noticed.

"You can't be everywhere," she warned one evening, watching men linger near the path Annajewel had taken. "They're starting to wait for you."

Annajewel rinsed her hands in the river, the cold water reddening her fingers. "I am not telling them to."

"That's worse," Nia said quietly.

Annajewel looked up. For a moment, something like confusion crossed her face—not fear, not pride. Calculation.

"They are tired," she said. "When people are tired, they stop choosing."

Nia followed her gaze across the camp. Men sat by cold fire pits, sharpening stakes. They watched her pass.

And when she disappeared into the trees, the camp sagged, as if a line had gone slack.

The tents were gray with mildew. The mud was black.

Annajewel walked through the perimeter. She carried a satchel of willow bark and dried mint. She walked with a long, eating stride.

The camp had changed in five years. The desperation had curdled into resentment.

Resentment needed a shape.

It found one in the pauses that followed her footsteps.

Men began to talk when she was not present. The words were cautious at first, wrapped in jokes that didn't land. Strange girl. Quiet one. Thinks she runs things. The phrases drifted through the camp like smoke, leaving no clear source.

A mercenary laughed too loudly one night and said she was putting a spell on them. No one laughed back. He drank harder after that, as if trying to burn something out of himself.

Others resisted in smaller ways. A man refused food she handed him and took it later from Nia instead, eyes down. A woman crossed herself when Annajewel passed, then pretended it was for the cold. Two brothers who had fought over blankets for weeks suddenly agreed she was dangerous—not because she harmed anyone, but because she made them feel watched.

Annajewel noticed none of it directly.

But she felt the edges tightening.

Paths altered around her. Voices lowered. People began standing with their backs to walls when she was near. Not out of fear—out of preparation.

One evening, as she walked past the fire ring, a miner muttered, "She thinks she's better than us."

Annajewel stopped.

The camp stilled.

She turned—not toward the man, but toward the fire. She crouched and adjusted a fallen log with careful hands, sending sparks up into the dark. When she stood again, she continued on without a word.

The miner flushed, unsure why his heart was pounding.

Later, he would tell himself he had won.

Later, he would not be able to explain why the fire burned more evenly after she touched it.

It showed in the way people watched her now.

In the early years, her arrival had brought relief. She had been the girl with food, the girl who organized, the girl who made the chaos pause long enough for breath to return. Gratitude had followed her like a shadow. Gratitude was manageable.

Resentment was not.

Men tracked her movements with narrowed eyes, counting what she carried and what she did not. Whispers moved through the camp faster than she did—questions about where the valley was, why some were fed and others turned away, why a girl barely grown had become the measure by which fairness was judged.

Need had hardened into expectation. Expectation had begun to rot.

Annajewel felt the shift but did not yet name it. She treated the camp the way she treated ailing soil: by correcting what could be corrected and ignoring the rest. But resentment, unlike hunger, did not lessen when fed. It only learned what it could demand next.

Men sat by cold fire pits, sharpening stakes. They watched her pass.

A soldier from the local garrison, a man named Hake, stepped into her path. He was young, bored, and leaning on a spear. He looked at the curve of her tunic where the wind pressed the fabric against her chest.

"Toll," Hake said. He grinned, showing a gap in his teeth.

Annajewel stopped. She looked at his hands. They were empty. She looked at his boots. The leather was split.

"I have no coin," she said.

Hake stepped closer. The smell of stale wine came off him in waves. "There are other ways to pay, girl. A pretty thing like you shouldn't be walking in the mud." He reached out, his fingers brushing the wool of her sleeve.

Annajewel looked at the hand on her arm. She saw the dirt under the fingernails. She saw the tremor in the thumb.

"You are shaking," she said.

Hake froze. The grin faltered. "What?"

"The fever," she said. She reached into her satchel and pulled out a strip of willow bark. She placed it in his hand. "Chew this. It stops the shaking."

She stepped around him.

Hake stood there, the bark in his palm. He looked at her back, then at the other men watching. He flushed a deep, angry red. He threw the bark into the mud.

"Witch," he muttered.

Nia was waiting by the riverbank. She looked older than her twenty-five years. Her hair was thinning, and her skin had the gray cast of chronic hunger.

"You shouldn't have come today," Nia whispered, taking the satchel.

"The fever doesn't know what day it is," Annajewel said, kneeling to check a sick child.

"It's the Day of Reflection, Anna," Nia hissed. "The soldiers are drunk. The priests are in the temples. The roads are empty."

Annajewel felt the child's forehead. Hot. Dry. She began to crush the mint. "Empty roads are faster."

"You don't understand," Nia said, gripping Annajewel's wrist. "They look at you. The men. They look at you like... like meat."

Annajewel looked up. She saw the camp. She saw the men sharpening stakes. She saw Hake staring at her from the perimeter.

She saw hunger. Not the hunger for bread, but a different,

sharper appetite. But she had fed hunger before. She had stopped bullies with apples. She had calmed wolves with silence.

"They are empty," Annajewel said, pulling her wrist free. "Empty things always stare."

"They aren't empty," Nia warned. "They are full of something bad."

Nia's words stayed with her as Annajewel moved through the camp, settling into the work she had come to do.

She treated the fever as she always had—cool water, bark for pain, quiet voices to keep the mind from racing ahead of the body. The sick responded. Children slept. Breathing eased. Order returned in small, fragile pockets. From the outside, it looked like success.

But Annajewel felt the strain beneath it.

Eyes followed her too closely. Conversations stopped when she knelt beside a pallet. Men who had once waited for instruction now lingered, as if weighing her against something unseen. The work still happened, but it no longer softened the edges. It merely delayed them.

She understood then what Nia had meant. Hunger could be fed. Pain could be eased. But whatever had settled into the camp had been growing in the absence of both, and it had learned to wear patience like a mask.

By the time Annajewel gathered her satchel to leave, the day felt heavier than when she had arrived, as if the air itself were holding its breath.

Annajewel left the camp an hour before sundown.

The sky was a bruised purple, heavy with unfallen snow. The Day of Reflection had drained the road of witnesses.

Annajewel had learned the rhythm of such days over the years. Bells rang in the towns. Priests spoke of humility and sacrifice to rooms already heavy with incense and wine. Men drank earlier than they should have and longer than they meant to. The world slowed its guard, mistaking ritual for safety.

The woods did not change for holy days. Birch bark gleamed pale and indifferent in the fading light. Snow hissed faintly underfoot where it had begun to crust. Every sound carried farther without the clutter of travel to soften it.

Annajewel adjusted her pace, lengthening her stride. Empty roads were faster, yes—but they were also exposed. She did not feel fear. She noted conditions. That was how she had always moved through danger: by acknowledging it and proceeding anyway.

When the twig snapped, it did not surprise her.

The wind cut through her cloak.

She took the shortcut through the Birch Wood. Kael watched from the ridge as her figure slipped between the pale trunks.

He told himself he was counting time. Measuring the distance. Making sure she reached the cabin before dark. But he stayed long after she vanished from sight.

It was a narrow track, flanked by white trees that looked like bone in the twilight. She walked quickly. Her mind was on the inventory—how much willow bark was left, how many apples remained in the cellar.

A twig snapped.

It wasn't a deer. Deer stepped with a distinct rhythm—step, pause, step. This was a heavy, dragging sound.

Annajewel stopped.

From behind a cluster of birches, three men stepped out. They wore the rusted chainmail of the garrison, but they had removed their crests. They wore hoods.

Hake was in the middle.

Annajewel turned. Two more men stepped out from the trees behind her. She was surrounded.

She stood still. She looked at them. She measured the distance. She measured the weight of the men.

"The toll," Hake said. His voice was thick, wet with the

anticipation of cruelty. "You forgot to pay the toll."

He held a knife. It was a long, serrated blade, more suited for sawing wood than fighting.

Annajewel looked at the knife. "I gave you the bark," she said calmly.

Hake laughed. It was a nervous sound. "We don't want bark." He stepped forward, the knife leveling at her chest. "We want what you're hiding under that cloak."

He lunged.

Annajewel didn't flinch, but she didn't have to fight.

Kael burst from the trees above the path. There was a sound like a falling tree—heavy, rushing air—followed by a sickening thud.

Kael hit Hake from the side.

It wasn't a duel. It was an impact. Kael, broad-shouldered and fueled by a father's terrifying rage, slammed into the soldier, driving him into the frozen earth. The knife flew from Hake's hand, spinning away into the snow.

Kael didn't stop. He grabbed Hake by the collar of his chainmail and hauled him up, slamming him back against the trunk of a birch tree. The wood groaned under the force.

"You touch her," Kael snarled, his face inches from Hake's, "and I will feed you to the roots piece by piece."

The other four men froze. They saw the axe in Kael's belt. They saw the murder in his eyes. They were bullies, not warriors, and bullies do not fight men who look ready to die.

"It... it was a joke," the scarred man stammered, backing away. "Just a toll, woodworker. Just a toll."

"Run," Kael roared.

They ran. Hake scrambled out of Kael's grip, falling in the snow, crawling on hands and knees until he regained his footing. They vanished into the gloom, the sound of their panicked retreat fading quickly.

Kael stood there, chest heaving, his breath steaming in the cold air. He turned to Annajewel. He grabbed her shoulders, his grip hard, checking her for cuts, for bruises.

"Are you hurt?" he demanded, his voice shaking.

"No, Papa," Annajewel said. She was calm. Too calm. She looked at the spot where Hake had fallen, then up at her father. "You were watching."

"Of course I was watching!" Kael shouted, the fear turning into anger. "The world is full of wolves, Anna! You cannot walk through it like it's a garden!"

"I handled it," she said softly.

"You stood there!" Kael let her go, running a hand through his white hair. "You stood there and let him point a knife at you. If I hadn't been on the ridge..."

He trailed off. The silence of the woods pressed in.

"If I hadn't been there," he whispered, the reality settling on him like a weight.

Annajewel adjusted her cloak. She picked up her satchel. "But you were there," she said.

Kael looked at her. He saw the copper fire of her hair hidden beneath the hood. He saw the daughter he had tried to hide behind brambles, behind walls, behind silence.

He realized then that his protection was the only thing keeping her alive. And he realized, with a cold dread that settled in his stomach, that he could not watch from the ridge forever.

"Come home," Kael said, his voice hollow. "Mara is waiting."

He walked behind her the rest of the way, his hand on his axe, eyes scanning the trees. He walked like a man who knew the storm was no longer coming, but had already arrived.

Chapter 7: The Rot in the Wood

Two winters passed, and the bruises of the world turned into scars.

Annajewel was seventeen. The awkward angles of childhood had smoothed out into a strength that was harder to hide. She moved with a fluid, efficient grace that drew eyes whenever she entered Oakhaven.

She wore her hood up, always. The hood did not make her invisible. If anything, it made her easier to track.

In Oakhaven, eyes followed patterns the way water followed grooves. People looked where noise was. Where violence lived. Where hunger argued with itself in the open. Annajewel moved against that current, and the town noticed without knowing how to articulate it.

She crossed the square and men shifted to give her room. Not quickly. Not fearfully. Just enough that she did not have to alter her stride.

By the time she reached the well, a small ring of space had formed around her. No one stepped into it. No one claimed it. It existed anyway.

Jace watched from the tannery wall, where the stink was strong enough to hide him.

He was twenty-one now, broad-shouldered and thick-necked. He wore a patchwork of stolen leather armor and carried a club weighted with iron nails. The limp Annajewel had given him years ago had settled into a permanent, grinding rhythm.

He watched her pump the water. Squeak. Splash. Squeak. Splash.

He hated the sound. But more than that, he hated the space around her.

"Look at her," Jace muttered to Rern and Silas, who lounged in the mud beside him. "Walking like she owns the stones."

"She's got the woodworker watching the ridge," Silas warned, spitting on the ground. "You heard about Hake. The father nearly took his head off."

"The father isn't here," Jace said, his eyes yellow and restless. "And Hake was a coward."

He pushed off the wall. The pain in his leg flared—a sharp, honest reminder of why he hated her. He limped into the sunlight.

Annajewel didn't stop pumping the water. She knew the sound of that limp. She had memorized it years ago in an alleyway.

"Leave some for the rest of us, Royalty," Jace sneered.

Annajewel stopped. She lifted the heavy clay jug, resting it on her hip. She turned to look at him. She didn't look at the club; she looked at his eyes.

"The water is free, Jace," she said. Her voice was calm, and it made his anger feel suddenly loud.

"Nothing is free," Jace stepped closer, invading her space. The smell of stale ale and rot hung on him. "You come down here every week with your baskets and your medicine. You think because you feed a few rats you're a saint?"

"I think I am thirsty," Annajewel said simply. "And I think you are bored."

She tried to step around him.

Jace moved, blocking her path. He didn't raise the club yet. He just used his bulk, leaning in.

"I'm not bored," he whispered, the bile rising in his throat. "I'm remembering. I remember a little girl with a stick. I remember a broken leg. It still aches when it rains, Anna."

"Pain is a teacher," Annajewel said, meeting his gaze. "But only if you listen."

Jace's face twisted. He hated her silence. He hated her calm.

But most of all, he hated that she wasn't afraid. He wanted to see her shake. He wanted to prove that the "Royalty" was just a mask.

He reached out, his hand hovering near her hood. "Maybe I should take a toll. A lock of that pretty hair to pay for the limp."

"Touch her, Jace, and you'll lose the hand."

The voice was lazy, dry, and came from the porch of the tavern across the square.

Jace froze. He looked over his shoulder.

Torian was leaning against a wooden post, peeling an apple with a long dagger. He was a Sergeant now, wearing the crimson cloak of the Red Cloaks, but he wore it with the indifference of a man who knew the uniform didn't matter.

Torian watched the square the way he watched terrain—without sentiment. He noted the gaps people left as she crossed. It looked, at a distance, like discipline.

"This is local business, Red Cloak," Jace growled, though he took a half-step back.

"It's boring business," Torian drawled, slicing a piece of apple. "And it's loud. I'm trying to enjoy my fruit."

He pointed the knife at Jace. "Walk away, cripple. Before I decide to even out your legs."

Jace's face went purple. He looked at Annajewel, then at Torian. He calculated the odds.

He realized the pattern. In the woods, the father. In the town, the soldier.

"You won't always have a guard dog, Royalty," Jace hissed at Annajewel, his voice dropping so only she could hear. "One day, the road will be empty. One day, the shepherds will be gone."

He signaled to Rern and Silas, and the three of them slunk back into the alley shadows.

Annajewel didn't watch them go. She turned to Torian.

The mercenary sheathed his dagger and took a bite of the apple.

He walked over to the well, his chainmail clinking softly.

"You have a bad habit of making enemies," Torian said, looking at the water jug. "Here. It's too heavy for you."

He reached for the jug.

"I can carry it," Annajewel said, hoisting it onto her shoulder with effortless strength.

Torian laughed, a short, sharp bark. "I know you can. I remember the alley. But Jace... he's rot. You can't fix it. You have to burn it out."

"He is a man," Annajewel said. "He has a soul."

"He has a grudge," Torian corrected, his eyes hard. "And grudges are heavier than water. Watch your back, girl. The Red Cloaks march north again in three days. The dogs will be off the leash."

Annajewel looked at him. She saw the exhaustion in his eyes. She saw a man who had seen too much blood and forgotten what it was like to build something.

"Thank you, Torian," she said.

Torian shrugged, looking uncomfortable. "Don't thank me. I just wanted quiet."

Annajewel turned and walked toward the orphanage, her back straight.

Torian watched her go. He touched the hilt of his sword. He thought of Jace's yellow eyes.

"She's going to get herself killed," Torian muttered to the empty square. "And she's going to forgive the bastard who does it."

Chapter 8: The Vigil

The Day of Reflection was meant for silence.

In Oakhaven, the shutters were closed. The smithy fire was doused. The Red Cloaks had marched north two days prior, leaving the town to its own hollow piety. The streets were empty, save for the wind pushing drifts of dry snow against the foundations.

The silence was not peace. It was suspension.

On ordinary days, Oakhaven breathed—voices calling, doors opening, boots scuffing mud. On the Day of Reflection, all of that was pressed flat beneath ritual. People stayed indoors not because they were holy, but because they were waiting for the day to end. Windows were shuttered against more than the cold. Confession was safer when it could not be overheard.

The absence of the Red Cloaks deepened it. Their marches had always been loud, deliberate, meant to be noticed. Without them, the town felt unguarded in a way that went beyond safety. The rules still existed, but no one was watching to see if they were kept.

Annajewel felt the difference as she stepped onto the high path. Silence like this did not protect. It created room.

Annajewel walked the high path. She carried no basket this time, only a small pouch of willow bark tucked into her belt. Nia had sent word at dawn—the fever had broken in the camp, but the coughing remained.

The woods were still. The birch trees stood like bone against the gray sky.

Stillness had learned her shape.

As Annajewel walked, the forest adjusted around her with the same unconscious courtesy the camp had shown. Snow slid from branches after she passed. A crow lifted from a stump and circled once before settling farther upslope. Even the wind seemed to thin, choosing paths that did not cross hers.

She noticed none of it.

Her mind was on inventories—how much bark remained, how many apples were left in the cellar, whether the winter would stretch another week. These were solvable problems. They kept the fear small.

At the bend in the path, she paused.

Not because she sensed danger. Because the quiet had changed.

It was not the attentive quiet that followed her steps. This was emptier. Hollow. As if something had stepped aside and not yet returned.

She waited. Counted three breaths. Then moved on.

Behind her, the woods closed again, obedient and blind.

Annajewel didn't scan the ridgeline. She didn't check for hawks. She was thinking of the inventory in the cellar, calculating how long the dried apples would last if the winter held for another month.

This was how she kept fear from taking root—by naming quantities, by measuring what remained.

She counted jars without seeing them, recalled which lids had warped and which seals still held. She adjusted for the extra mouths at the bridge and the loss that came with every distribution. Hunger could be managed if it was faced directly. Winter could be endured if it was accounted for early enough.

The habit had become armor. When her thoughts were ordered, her body followed. When her body followed, the world tended to make room.

She did not notice how alone the path had become until it bent ahead of her, the old stone marker rising out of the snow like a warning no one remembered how to read.

She rounded the bend near the old stone marker.

Three figures blocked the path.

They didn't step out from trees. They didn't jump. They were simply standing there, waiting, as if they were part of the landscape that had rotted.

For a heartbeat, the old pattern tried to assert itself.

Rern shifted his weight without meaning to, boots scraping in the snow. Silas swallowed, his grip tightening on nothing. Even Jace hesitated, his breath hitching as if the ground beneath him had tilted.

Annajewel felt it—the familiar thinning of the air, the subtle pull that made men pause and reconsider. She met Jace's eyes and saw the flicker of recognition there. Not remorse. Memory.

It should have been enough.

It wasn't.

The moment broke from the stillness they had created as Jace leaned into his bad leg and felt the pain spike. The ache anchored him. It reminded him who he was supposed to be. His mouth twisted, and the hesitation burned off, replaced by something sharper and more determined.

"Not today," he said, more to himself than to her.

He stepped forward, and the others followed.

The woods did not intervene. The snow did not shift. Whatever had once made space for her had reached its limit.

Magnetism could stall indecision.

It could not stop intent.

Jace stood in the center. Rern and Silas flanked him. They wore heavy cloaks, but their heads were bare. The cold had turned their faces raw and red.

Annajewel stopped.

She looked at Jace. She didn't look at the club in his hand. She looked at his posture. He was leaning forward, weight on his good leg, vibrating with a tension that had nothing to do with the cold.

"The road is closed," Jace said.

His voice was thin, snatched away by the wind.

"I am going to the bridge," Annajewel said. She didn't step back. She didn't step forward. She stood.

"No," Jace said. He took a step. The club tapped against his thigh. "You aren't going anywhere, Royalty. The toll is due."

Rern and Silas fanned out, moving into the deep snow to flank her. They moved clumsily, their boots crunching loud in the silence. They were smiling, but the smiles didn't reach their eyes. Their eyes were flat, glassy with adrenaline and bad intent.

"Torian is gone," Silas mocked, his voice cracking. "No guard dogs today."

Annajewel watched them close the circle. She saw the logic of it. They had waited for the holiday. They had waited for the soldiers to leave. They had waited for the silence.

"You are cold," Annajewel observed. "Go home, Jace."

Jace flinched. The concern in her voice hit him like a slap. He didn't want her pity. He wanted her fear. He needed her to be small so he could finally feel big.

"Shut up," he hissed. "Don't you talk down to me. Not today."

He lunged.

It wasn't a fight. A fight implies two sides trying to win.

What followed had none of the balance she had learned to read.

There was no exchange, no rhythm to catch and turn. The men moved together, crowding space, taking advantage of weight and number rather than skill. Snow muffled their footing, robbed her of leverage, turned instinct into liability. This was not conflict as correction. It was force applied until something gave.

Annajewel felt the shift immediately. In the alley years ago, violence had been sharp and brief, a problem solved and set aside. Here, it stretched, clumsy and relentless. Every motion carried intent but no purpose, each blow driven less by strategy than by the need to feel something break.

She understood then what had changed. The men were not trying to stop her. They were trying to erase her—proof that their world had ever bent around something better than them.

The realization did not frighten her.

It clarified.

This was an erasure.

Annajewel moved to deflect, her hand coming up to catch his wrist. But the snow was slick. Her foot slipped on a patch of ice.

Balance failed.

Jace's club didn't hit her head. It hit her shoulder.

The sound was dull, like an axe hitting wet wood.

Annajewel went down. The pain was sudden and white, wiping out the world for a heartbeat. She hit the frozen ground, the air driven from her lungs.

Before she could rise, weight fell on her. Heavy, smelling of stale wool and sweat.

They stumbled downhill, boots slipping in the snow, until her back struck the roots of a great oak.

Rern pinned her legs. Silas grabbed her arms.

Jace stood over her. He was breathing hard, clouds of steam puffing from his mouth. He looked down at her, expecting to see terror. He wanted her to beg. He wanted to hear the "Royalty" crack.

Annajewel looked up. Her hood had fallen back. Her hair spilled across the snow, the copper dark against the white.

She looked at him. Her eyes were clear. She saw the rage in him, but she also saw the terrifying emptiness beneath it. He was a boy breaking a toy because he didn't know how to build anything.

"Jace," she whispered.

It wasn't a plea. It was a naming.

Jace screamed. It was a sound of pure frustration. He couldn't break the look in her eyes, so he decided to break the eyes themselves.

He dropped the club. He used his fists.

The violence was messy. It lacked the precision of the alleyway years ago. It was desperate, frantic work. They hit her until their hands hurt. They tore the wool tunic. They struck until the copper hair was matted with mud and darker things.

Through it all, the woods remained silent. The birch trees did not bend. The wind did not howl. The world simply watched, indifferent to the breaking of one girl.

When they were done, they stood back, panting.

Annajewel lay in the snow. She didn't move. One arm was bent wrong. Her face was a ruin.

Jace looked at his hands. They were shaking. He looked at her, waiting for the satisfaction to hit him. He waited for the rush of power.

It didn't come.

Instead, he felt a sudden, crushing nausea. He looked at the girl in the snow and realized she looked exactly the same as she had standing up—unconquered. He hadn't taken her dignity. He had only taken her breath.

"She's dead," Rern whispered, backing away, his face pale. "You killed her, Jace."

"Shut up," Jace gasped. He looked around the empty woods. "Leave her. The wolves will take care of it."

They ran. They scrambled back down the path, slipping in the snow, fleeing from the stillness they had created.

The woods did not answer.

Snow continued to fall with patient indifference, settling into the churned tracks and broken crust. The marks of boots softened. The sound of their flight thinned and vanished. No branch snapped in pursuit. No bird took alarm.

Annajewel lay where she had fallen, the heat leaving her body in slow, measurable stages. The ground beneath her accepted the weight without comment. It had accepted worse.

Somewhere deeper in the forest, an animal paused at the edge of the clearing, then moved on. Hunger had rules. This did not belong to them.

The stillness returned—not the attentive stillness that had followed her steps, but the older kind. The kind that waits.

Nothing rose up to correct what had been done.

Nothing came.

Annajewel was not dead.

Pain was a country, and she was exploring its borders. It was cold there.

She couldn't feel her legs. Her shoulder throbbed with a heavy, rhythmic dullness. She tried to take a breath, but her ribs grated together, stopping the air halfway.

She opened her eyes.

The sky was graying toward twilight. A single star had appeared through the clouds.

She tried to move her hand. Her fingers brushed against something rough. Bark.

She lay at the base of a massive oak tree at the edge of the clearing. Its roots broke the surface of the snow like the knuckles of an old man.

She rested her head against the wood.

It was quiet.

She thought of Kael. He would be checking the brambles, waiting for her. She thought of Mara, counting the apples. She thought of Nia, waiting at the bridge.

She felt a tear leak from her eye. It cut a warm track through the blood on her cheek.

She didn't cry for the pain. The pain was just a signal that the body was ending.

She cried for Jace.

She closed her eyes and saw his face as he stood over her. She saw the yellow fear in his eyes. He had ruined his own soul to break her body. It was a terrible trade.

They are empty, she thought. They are so hungry.

The cold began to move inward. It started in her toes and crept up her spine. It wasn't unpleasant. It felt like sinking into the stream on a hot day.

She pressed her cheek against the rough bark of the tree. The earth smelled of iron and sleep.

I am done, she whispered to the roots. I am tired.

The earth did not answer with words. It answered with gravity. It seemed to pull at her, welcoming the weight.

The snow began to fall again. Large, soft flakes that covered the red stains on her tunic. They settled on her eyelashes. They settled on her hair.

Her breathing slowed. Shallow. Hitching. Then, nothing.

The woods held the silence.

Beneath the snow, where her blood touched the soil, the roots of the great tree drank. They pulled the copper warmth down, deep into the frost line, locking it away.

Beneath the snow, where her blood touched the soil, warmth bled into the frozen earth.

High above, in the canopy, a single dead leaf did not fall. It darkened to bronze. Then another. Then another—metallic against the gray sky.

The tree stood in the dark.

Chapter 9: After the Snow

The lantern carved a small, yellow sphere out of the night. Beyond that edge, the valley was a throat of darkness.

Kael stood at the bramble gate. The snow had stopped falling, but the wind was drifting it, erasing the world one inch at a time. He held the lantern high, the oil sloshing in the tank.

He wasn't waiting anymore. He was vibrating. Waiting had stopped behaving.

Time stretched, then folded in on itself. Kael checked the lantern oil twice, then forgot he had done so and checked again. The light wavered, smearing the bramble shadows into shapes that meant nothing. He tried to name the sounds of the night—wind, snow, branch—but every noise arrived stripped of certainty.

Mara stood in the doorway, unmoving. She did not ask questions anymore. Questions implied answers, and answers implied a shape the night had not yet given her. She watched Kael's back, the way his shoulders held themselves too high, as if braced for impact.

"She knows the path," Mara said finally. It wasn't reassurance. It was inventory.

Kael nodded once. He did not trust his voice.

The wind shifted. Snow rattled against the cabin wall. Somewhere below the ridge, a fox cried out—a thin, cutting sound that made Mara's hands curl into fists.

Kael raised the lantern higher.

Nothing answered.

Kael had learned the difference between patience and knowledge.

Patience waited. Knowledge calculated. Knowledge marked

time not by hope but by deviation. Every step Annajewel took had weight and measure. Every journey she made followed a rhythm he could feel in his bones. Tonight, the rhythm had broken.

He lifted the lantern higher, angling it toward the ridge as if light itself might summon her. The flame guttered, stretched thin by the wind, and he cupped a hand around the glass without realizing his fingers were burning.

Something was wrong. Not the weather. Not the hour. Her absence itself had mass.

Kael did not say her name again. Saying it felt like tempting the dark to answer.

"Kael."

Mara stood in the doorway of the cabin, fifty paces back. She wasn't wearing her cloak. She was shivering, her arms wrapped around her chest. "Come inside. She is just... delayed. The snow is deep."

Kael didn't answer. He knew the rhythm of his daughter's walk. He knew how long it took to cross the ridge. He knew that Annajewel did not delay.

He pushed through the brambles. The thorns snagged his coat, but he tore free, stepping out onto the deer trail.

"Go back inside, Mara," he called over his shoulder. His voice sounded thin, swallowed instantly by the trees. "Keep the fire up."

He didn't wait for her to answer. He started to climb.

He met Nia half a mile up the ridge.

The apprentice was stumbling down the path, sliding on the ice. She had no lantern. When she saw Kael's light, she didn't run toward it. She stopped. She looked like a deer caught in the open— frozen, trembling.

Kael raised the light. He saw her face. It was gray with cold and wet with tears.

"Where is she?" Kael asked.

Nia shook her head. Her teeth were chattering too hard for words.

Kael stepped forward, gripping her shoulder. "Nia. Where is Anna?"

"She never came," Nia choked out. "I waited. The sun went down. She never came."

The lantern swung in Kael's hand, shadows jumping wildly against the trees.

"She left at noon," Kael said. He was pleading with the math. "She took the high path."

"I checked the high path," Nia sobbed. "I shouted for her. There's nothing, Kael. Just snow."

Kael shoved past her. He didn't run—the ground was too treacherous—but he moved fast, reckless. Nia followed, stepping into the holes his boots punched into the drifts.

They reached the bend near the stone marker.

Kael lowered the lantern.

The snow here was wrong.

Snow remembered disturbance longer than earth did.

Where feet had slid, the crust lay shattered into dull plates. Where weight had fallen, the powder was pressed flat, its surface glazed and darkened by warmth that had no business being there anymore. Even as the wind worked to soften the damage, it could not erase the story entirely.

Kael knelt, holding the lantern close. The light picked out lines that ran downhill instead of along the path, marks that spoke of struggle rather than travel. This was not the passing mess of an animal or a careless step in the dark. This was intent made visible.

He followed it without speaking, letting the ground tell him what no voice could.

It was churned and scuffed, a mess of slides and broken crust being slowly erased by the wind.

"Here," Kael whispered.

He followed the marks off the path, down the shallow slope toward the trees.

The light caught the base of a massive oak.

The tree looked wrong.

Not damaged. Not broken. Simply present in a way the rest of the forest was not. Its trunk absorbed the lantern light instead of reflecting it, the bark dull and dark, swallowing yellow into itself.

Kael took one step forward.

Then he saw her hand.

It lay palm-up in the snow, fingers slightly curled, as if still holding something small and essential. The skin was already losing its color, the cold drawing the life inward.

He stopped moving.

The world narrowed to detail. The bent angle of her arm. The dark smear at her temple. The way her braid had come loose, copper threads tangled with frost.

"Anna," he said.

The name did not behave like a word. It fell, struck the ground, and stayed there.

He knelt beside her. His knees soaked through immediately, but the cold did not register. He brushed snow from her cheek with the back of his hand. The skin was firm. Not rigid. But unmistakably wrong.

Behind him, Nia made a sound and then bit it back. She pressed her fist into her mouth, hard enough to draw blood.

Kael leaned closer, as if proximity could alter the outcome. He pressed his ear to her chest, counting without knowing what he was counting for.

One.

Two.

Nothing.

He did not collapse. He did not cry out.

He sat back on his heels and stared at the place where breath should have been.

"I was late," he said.

No one answered.

Annajewel lay at its roots.

She was half-covered by snow, her dark hair spread against the white. One arm lay bent at an angle that made Kael's stomach lurch. Her face was bruised and swollen, barely recognizable.

Kael dropped to his knees.

"Anna," he said, and the name came out broken.

He brushed snow from her cheek with shaking fingers. Her skin was cold. Not chilled—cold. He pressed his ear to her chest anyway, as if the night might have lied.

It had not.

Nia stood behind him, her hands clasped to her mouth. She didn't step closer. She already knew.

They stayed like that for a long time, neither of them speaking, the lantern guttering in the wind. Time lost its usefulness beside her.

The wind moved snow across her body with a gentleness that felt obscene, as if the night were trying to finish what the men had begun by erasing the evidence. Kael brushed it away again and again, not because it mattered, but because stopping would have meant accepting what his hands already knew.

Nia sank down onto the frozen ground a few paces back. She pressed her fists into her mouth to keep from making noise. Sound felt like a betrayal. The valley had raised them to endure quietly, and grief obeyed the same rule.

Kael traced the outline of Annajewel's braid where it lay against the white. He did not try to straighten her arm. He did not try to close her eyes. Those were tasks for a future that no longer existed.

When he finally stood, it was not because he was ready, but because the cold had begun to claim decisions for him.

The cold deepened.

Kael straightened at last.

"We can't leave her," he said. His voice was flat, already emptied. "The ground will freeze by morning."

They worked without speaking.

The earth fought them. The iron rang once against the frost and bent uselessly. Kael dropped the tool and dug with his hands instead, tearing through roots and frozen soil until his fingers split and bled.

They wrapped Annajewel in her cloak and laid her where she had fallen.

No prayers. No words.

They pulled the earth back over her, pressing it down with numb boots as snow began to fall again, soft and patient, erasing the work of their hands.

Kael remained standing long after they were finished, blood darkening the snow, unable to remember when he had stopped digging.

Above them, the oak still held its leaves. That alone was wrong. They were dark now—darker than they should have been—but in the lantern light they might have been only wet, only heavy with frost.

Kael did not touch them.

The walk back to the cabin was silent.

Mara opened the door before they reached the porch. She looked at Kael's face. She looked at the space beside him.

She didn't scream. She simply exhaled, a long, shuddering breath, as if something vital had left her.

Kael walked past her into the cabin. He set the lantern on the table.

"She's gone," he said.

Mara made a sound that was not a word and folded against the wall.

Nia stood in the doorway, unable to enter, unable to leave.

Kael looked at the corner of the room.

The oak cradle he had built years ago sat there, filled with kindling. Strong. Careful. Useless.

"Close the door," Kael said.

"But if she comes back—" Mara whispered.

"She isn't," Kael said, and his voice broke. "Close it. The wind is cold."

He crossed the room and slid the iron bolt home.

Thud.

The sound echoed in the cabin. It did not sound like safety.

It sounded like something sealed.

Chapter 10: The Root and the Rust

Winter did not end; it merely rotted.

The valley did not thaw evenly.

Patches of frost clung to the ground in places the sun reached first, while other stretches collapsed into mud overnight. Trees budded late or not at all. The birds returned in smaller numbers, circling the orchard without landing, as if unsure where the ground truly was.

People said it was a hard winter lingering.

But the earth did not feel tired.

It felt changed.

The season loosened its grip without releasing what it had taken.

Ice withdrew from the ground in reluctant sheets, leaving behind water that had nowhere to go. Roads softened into traps. Fields exhaled the smells they had sealed away—animal fat, spoiled grain, and the quiet corruption of shallow graves disturbed by thaw. Spring did not arrive as renewal. It arrived as exposure.

In Oakhaven, people called this mercy. The priests rang bells and spoke of forgiveness while boots sank ankle-deep in what winter had preserved. Men stepped carefully, not out of reverence, but because rot had a way of catching the unwary.

Nia felt it under her feet as she climbed the ridge. Whatever had been buried was not staying buried.

The thaw came to Oakhaven in March, turning the frozen ruts of the trade road into sucking trenches of mud. The snow receded unevenly, peeling back like a bandage from a dirty wound to reveal what had been hidden for months: the carcasses of livestock that hadn't survived the frost, broken cart wheels, and the shallow graves of those who couldn't pay the temple tax.

Nia walked the ridge line. The air smelled of wet wool and decomposition.

Nia noticed it first.

She had lived her life by small changes—the color of a tongue in fever, the smell of rot before it showed. On her walks along the ridge, she began to feel watched, not by eyes, but by weight. The ground pressed differently beneath her boots near the clearing, firmer, almost reluctant to yield.

When she stopped, the silence thickened.

It was not absence of sound. It was restraint.

She found herself holding her breath without knowing why.

She hadn't been to the valley in weeks. The path was treacherous, slick with meltwater that ran down the rock face in gray sheets. She kept her head down, watching her boots sink into the sludge.

She told herself she was going to check on Mara. She told herself she was bringing news of the Iron Empire's movements—the rumors that General Valerius had taken the northern pass.

She didn't tell herself the truth: that she was counting the days.

Ninety days since the snow fell. Ninety days since they had turned the earth.

She reached the bramble gate. It was overgrown, the dead vines from last year tangled with new, pale green shoots. Kael hadn't pruned it.

She pushed through.

The valley was waking up. The stream, swollen with runoff, roared over its banks, churning brown and angry. The apple trees were beginning to bud, small knots of green pushing through the bark.

Everything was moving. Everything was softening.

Except that some things did not soften.

Nia felt it in her joints first—a faint resistance, as if the valley itself were bracing. The air near the clearing carried a subtle tang she could not name, not rot, not rain. Something metallic. Old. Patient.

She slowed without deciding to. Her steps shortened. Her hand hovered near her chest, fingers curling as though around an absent charm.

The world had not frozen.

It had set.

Except the Oak.

It did not dominate the clearing.

It did not loom.

It waited.

The trunk was darker than memory allowed, the bark neither cracked nor living, but sealed—smooth in places where age should have split it. The leaves hung heavy and dull, catching no light, as if they absorbed it rather than reflected it.

Nia had the sudden, irrational certainty that the tree was not growing upward.

It was growing inward.

It did not participate in the season.

Where the rest of the valley softened—buds swelling, bark loosening, water moving freely—the Oak held itself apart, unchanged and unmoved. It did not sag with meltwater or shiver in the breeze. It stood as it had in winter, rigid and unyielding, as if time itself had glanced off it and moved on.

Nia had walked this path since she was a girl. She knew how the valley breathed, how trees responded when the frost finally let go. This was wrong in a way that had nothing to do with disease or neglect. It felt intentional.

The Oak did not look sick. It looked decided.

Nia stopped at the bend. She didn't want to look, but her eyes went to it like a tongue finding a missing tooth.

The great tree at the edge of the clearing stood apart.

The snow around its base had melted, revealing the disturbed earth of the mound. But the canopy was wrong. Every other tree in the valley was bare, waiting for spring. The Oak still held its leaves.

They weren't green. They weren't the brown of dead foliage that clings through winter. They were a dull, heavy gray, slick with rain. They hung straight down, motionless in the breeze that shook the rest of the orchard.

Kael was there.

Nia almost didn't recognize him.

Grief had thinned him, drawn the skin tight across his face as if the winter had tried to pull him inside out. He stood too close to the tree, not reverent, not fearful—just stubborn, as though proximity itself were an argument.

He hadn't come to mourn.

He had come to correct something.

He was standing knee-deep in the mud near the trunk. He held a hand axe. He looked thinner, his beard gray and unkempt. He wasn't looking at the mound; he was looking at a low-hanging branch that obscured the view of the mound.

The branch hadn't grown there by accident.

It bent inward, heavy and deliberate, as if the tree itself had chosen to hide what lay beneath it.

Kael's jaw tightened.

If the earth insisted on covering her, then he would insist on seeing her.

Nia stepped forward, her boots squelching. "Kael?"

He didn't jump. He didn't turn. He just lifted the axe.

"It's in the way," Kael muttered. His voice was rusty, unused.

"I can't see the marker."

He swung the axe.

It wasn't a violent swing, just the practiced motion of a woods-man clearing a limb.

Clang.

The sound carried farther than it should have.

It rang through the valley like a struck bell, sharp and accusing, refusing to be absorbed by the damp air.

Kael felt it in his teeth.

The sound was wrong. It wasn't the dull thud of steel biting into wood.

The vibration ran up the handle and into Kael's bones.

It was a ringing protest, sharp and clean, the kind of sound meant to come from forges and anvils, not from living things. The branch did not flex. It did not splinter. It absorbed the blow and returned it, as if the tree were answering in a language Kael did not know how to speak.

He had cut oak his entire life. He knew the resistance of green wood, the stubborn bite of old growth, the brittle snap of winter-killed limbs. This was none of those. This was refusal.

For a moment, the valley seemed to hold its breath. Even the stream's roar softened, as if listening. Kael stared at the branch, the chipped blade, the impossible stillness, and felt the ground beneath him lose a rule he had trusted since boyhood.

Wood should yield. Steel should cut.

Something had reversed the order.

It was the high, ringing vibration of metal striking stone.

The axe bounced.

Kael stumbled back, the handle vibrating in his grip. He looked at the blade. The axe felt wrong in his hands—too light, as if the weight had shifted somewhere else. The edge was chipped, a jagged notch taken out of the steel.

He looked at the branch. The bark had flexed beneath the blow, not splintered—absorbing the strike the way packed earth absorbs rain.

There was no cut. There was no white wood exposed beneath the bark. There was only a shallow dent, dark and bruised. The branch had yielded just enough to remember the blow.

Nia felt a cold prickle at the base of her neck. The sound had traveled through her bones before it reached her ears. "The wood is frozen," she said quickly. "The sap is hard."

Kael frowned. He touched the branch. "It's fifty degrees, Nia. The mud is soup. The wood shouldn't be frozen."

He struck it again. Harder this time.

Clang.

The sound echoed through the quiet valley, harsh and dissonant. It sounded like a hammer hitting an anvil.

Kael dropped the axe. He backed away, rubbing his hand. "It won't cut," he whispered. "Why won't it cut?"

Nia walked to the tree. She reached out, hesitating, then touched a leaf.

It didn't crumble. It didn't bend. It felt stiff, heavy, and cold. The surface wasn't waxy like a leaf; it was rough, like rust.

"It's dead," Nia said, pulling her hand back. "It must be petrified. The soil... maybe the soil is bad."

She looked down at the grave. She thought of what lay beneath that soil. She thought of the blood that had soaked into the roots.

"It's just wood, Kael," she insisted, her voice rising. "It's just old, hard wood."

Even as she said it, the words sounded thin, like excuses spoken aloud to make them real.

Kael looked at her. His eyes were hollow. He didn't see a miracle. He saw a frustration. He saw a world that wouldn't even let him tend his daughter's grave properly.

"It ruins the view," he said helplessly. "I just wanted to clear the view."

Nia didn't stay long. The air in the valley felt heavy, pressurized.

She walked back to Oakhaven, the sound of that clang replaying in her mind.

She went straight to the old temple district, to the workshop of Tobin, the ironmonger. The forge was cold—fuel was scarce— but Tobin was there, repairing a plowshare.

"Tobin," Nia asked, standing in the doorway. "If an oak tree... if it won't cut. If the axe bounces."

Tobin didn't look up from his filing. "Frozen heartwood. Happens in the deep winter."

"But it's spring," Nia said. "And the leaves... they feel like lead."

Tobin snorted. He wiped grease from his hands with a rag. "Rot, then. Sometimes a tree dies standing up, and the rot hardens the core before it crumbles. Or lightning. Lightning cooks the sap, turns it to glass."

"Could it be..." Nia hesitated. She didn't know what she wanted to ask. "Could it be the ground? Something in the ground?"

Tobin looked at her then. He saw the fear in her eyes. He laughed, a harsh, cynical bark.

"Listen to me, girl. Wood is wood. Iron is iron. Trees don't turn into shields just because you want them to. If your axe is bouncing, sharpen your axe."

He threw the rag onto the bench.

"Now move along. Unless you have coin for nails, I have work to do."

Nia walked out into the mud.

She looked up at the ridge line, obscured by gray mist.

Wood is wood, she repeated to herself. Iron is iron.

But she looked at her own hand, the one that had touched the leaf. Her fingertips smelled faint, metallic.

It smelled like old pennies. The scent clung, sharp and stubborn, refusing to fade the way sap or soil should have.

She wiped her hand on her tunic, scrubbing hard, trying to get the smell off. She walked faster, head down, vanishing into the gray shuffle of the town. She didn't want to know. She wanted it to be rot. She wanted it to be lightning.

Because if it wasn't rot, and if it wasn't lightning, then the earth was doing something it wasn't supposed to do. And in Oakhaven, when the rules broke, people died.

Chapter 11: The Courtroom

There was no transition. No tunnel of light. No choir.

One moment she was cold, her cheek pressed to the rough bark of the oak. The next, she was kneeling on stone smoother than glass and warmer than blood.

The pain was gone. The shoulder that had been crushed felt whole. The ribs were silent.

Annajewel stood.

She was in a hall. Vast. The ceiling vanished into a height the eye could not measure. Scale asserted itself before authority did.

The space did not intimidate by threat or ornament. There were no banners, no thrones, no carved laws announcing consequence. The vastness existed only to remind her that she was not its measure. She felt neither welcomed nor barred. She felt placed.

The pillars of light were not structures but positions—fixed points where judgment could occur without obstruction. Nothing hid here. Nothing echoed. Even her breathing felt accounted for, as if the hall already knew how much air she required.

Annajewel understood, without instruction, that this was not a place of persuasion. It was a place of accounting. Intent weighed as much as action. Silence carried meaning.

She straightened, small within it, and waited to be addressed.

There were no walls—only pillars of white light falling from darkness above. The air smelled of nothing at all, like a page before ink.

She looked down. The wool tunic remained, but the stains were gone. The mud was gone. She was clean.

"Annajewel."

The voice did not come from a body. It came from the center of the space. It was not loud, but it struck through her, resonant and absolute, like a gavel finding its mark.

She walked forward. A dais waited there—plain, unadorned.

She did not know who spoke. Only that she was expected to answer.

"I am here," she said. Her voice sounded small.

"You have arrived early," the Voice said. Not accusation. Observation. "The thread was cut before the pattern was finished."

"I did not cut it."

"No. It was cut for you."

Light shifted between the pillars. Not scenes, but fragments—snow, the falling club, Jace's face warped with fear, hands pinning her to the ground.

"We have seen the act," the Voice said. "The violation is recorded. The debt is calculated."

The air thickened. Justice pressed in—cold, precise, unyielding.

"Name them," the Voice commanded. "Speak the names of those who broke the vessel. Their threads will be burned. This is the law of the Court."

Annajewel felt the expectation settle. Balance demanded balance. Blood for blood.

The demand was not emotional. It was structural.

This place did not rage. It did not pity. It corrected. Harm introduced imbalance, and imbalance required resolution. Threads were severed here with the same indifference a mason applied to flawed stone. Not because the stone was evil, but because it weakened the wall.

Annajewel felt how easily it could be done. A name spoken aloud would be enough. The law did not require hatred, only identification. Justice would proceed cleanly, efficiently, and without residue.

For a moment, she understood the appeal of it. How simple the world could be if pain were answered with erasure. How quiet.

The thought did not tempt her.

It clarified what she had already chosen.

She thought of Jace.

Not the man over her in the snow—but the boy in the alley, humiliated by a stick. A man so terrified of his own smallness that he tried to destroy what reminded him of it.

She thought of Oakhaven. Of hunger. Of rot that hollowed men until cruelty felt like survival.

Her throat tightened.

Grief.

She fell to her knees.

"Why do you kneel?" the Voice asked. "You are the injured. Stand and accuse."

She shook her head. Tears struck the stone—hot, real.

"They were hungry," she whispered.

"They were cruel."

"They were empty," she said. "They thought if they broke me, something would spill out that would fill them. It didn't."

"And for this, you weep?"

"I weep for them, for their souls." She looked up. "My pain is finished. But they must wake tomorrow. They must remember."

Silence filled the hall—stunned, unprepared. This place was built to sort right from wrong. Not this.

"You ask for no punishment?"

"I ask for forgiveness," Annajewel said. "Give them time."

Light intensified. It narrowed to her, examining the weight she carried.

"You are strange," the Voice said. "Most arrive light.

You arrive burdened."

Pressure increased.

"You have brought the world with you."

"It is heavy."

"It is too heavy. This place is for those who have let go."

Annajewel stood. She understood. This hall did not need her.

Oakhaven did.

"I cannot stay."

"No," the Voice agreed. "Gravity binds you. Your love anchors you to the earth."

The hall began to dim. The scent of iron and wet soil crept in.

"You will return."

Annajewel lifted her head. "To do what?"

The light shifted. Not images—weight.

"I don't know how."

"You will."

Understanding pressed into her—not instruction, not prophecy, but orientation.

Where cruelty gathered, she must stand.

Where hunger hollowed men, she must remain whole.

Where men stand empty, she shall guide them toward fullness.

Where the world broke itself trying to be strong, she must endure. The knowledge settled like gravity.

The floor dissolved. She was falling—not down, but inward. Into dark. Into cold. Into waiting wood.

"How long?" she called.

"Until the weight is gone."

Silence closed around her—not the silence of judgment, but of sap. Slow. Patient.

A tree waiting for the sun.

Chapter 12: The Hardening

Year One

The truth did not survive the winter. Truth required witnesses. Winter had taken most of them.

Snow erased tracks. Cold drove people inward, into taverns and kitchens where stories fermented faster than facts. By spring, what remained of Annajewel existed only as absence, and absence invited invention.

The valley did not help. It offered no answers, no signs that could be pointed to with certainty. There was only a mound of disturbed earth beneath a tree no one wished to name aloud. Without proof, grief loosened its grip on reality.

What could not be carried cleanly was reshaped until it fit the hands of those telling it.

By the time the snow melted into the gray slush of March, the story of Annajewel had rotted into a dozen conflicting lies.

In the taverns of Oakhaven, the men said she had run off with a soldier. In the washhouses, the women whispered that the father had gone mad and buried her alive to save food. The children said the wolves took her and raised her as one of their own.

Nia heard them all. She said nothing. She knew that people filled the silence with noise because the truth—that a girl had simply walked into the woods and died for nothing—was too heavy to carry.

The clearing became a place to be avoided. People did not agree on why—only that standing there made the chest feel heavier than it should. The deer trails that used to cross the orchard now diverted sharply into the brambles. The birds refused to land on the branches of the great Oak.

Kael still went to the clearing every day.

He did not stand beneath the tree as one stands with the dead. He stood as one waits for something unfinished to speak.

He did not kneel. He did not pray. He no longer brought tools.

He stood at the edge of the mound, staring at the black bark, waiting for a movement that never came.

Mara stopped speaking the name. She moved through the cabin like a draft—cooking, sweeping, counting apples—but she never looked at the door. To speak the name was to acknowledge the empty chair.

Grief did not fade in the valley. It calcified. It settled into people the way silt settles in a riverbed—slow, invisible, and impossible to wash out once it hardened. It hardened into habit.

People learned where not to walk, which conversations to shorten, which questions to swallow before they formed. The clearing became a boundary not marked on any map, but everyone felt it when they drew too close—a pressure behind the eyes, a tightening in the chest that warned them to turn aside.

Kael's grief settled into routine. He rose at the same hour each morning. He stood at the same distance from the mound. He left at the same time, as if obeying a rule written somewhere beneath the soil. Mara's grief took another shape. It hollowed her, leaving the shell of motion without intent.

Nothing healed. Nothing broke further. The valley learned to live around the wound, and in doing so, ensured it would never close.

Year Two

By the second autumn, the tree had become a problem. Not because it threatened them—but because it refused to change when everything else did.

It wasn't glowing. It wasn't splitting. It was simply... wrong.

The leaves didn't fall. They did not curl, yellow, or surrender to the season. They endured—heavy, inert, as if the tree had decided that time itself would move around it. While the rest of the orchard turned bare and gray, the copper canopy remained heavy and dark.

Kael tried to clear the brush that was creeping toward the mound. He swung his scythe, the blade flashing in the sun.

Clink.

The blade struck a protruding root. It didn't chip wood; the steel edge rolled as if it had hit granite. The handle cracked in Kael's hands.

He left the tool where it lay. He didn't tell Nia. He simply stopped clearing the brush.

A week later, a boy from the orphanage—a brave, foolish child named Tom—climbed the ridge on a dare. He did not climb out of cruelty. He climbed because the silence around the tree felt like a challenge, and children have always mistaken stillness for safety. He wanted a souvenir from the "Wolf Girl's" woods.

He stood under the great Oak. The lowest branches were just out of reach, heavy with dark, metallic foliage.

Tom jumped. His fingers closed around a leaf, and he yanked, expecting it to snap free like a twig.

He cried out.

He came running back to town, his hand dripping blood. The leaf hadn't torn. It hadn't even budged. The edge was rigid and sharp as a razor, and when he pulled against it, it had sliced his palm to the bone.

Nia bandaged the hand. She looked at the cut. It was clean and deep, the kind of wound made by a soldier's blade.

"Don't go back," she told the boy.

"It bit me," the boy sobbed. "I tried to pick it, and it bit me."

"That tree is protective, Tom," Nia said quietly. "Let it be."

Year Four

The path to the ridge had changed.

It was no longer the faint deer trail Kael had hidden with brambles. It was a scar. Thousands of feet—boots, bare soles, the dragging limp of the sick—had churned the mud until the earth refused to heal.

Nia paused at the bend, leaning heavily on her ash-wood cane. The climb was harder this year. Her knees complained with a dry, grinding ache that mirrored the mood of the town below.

"Go back, Nia," she whispered to herself, the steam of her breath snatching the words away. "There is nothing up there but wood and rot."

But she didn't go back. She was the keeper of the story, and stories required inspection.

She rounded the final turn into the clearing and stopped dead.

The great Oak did not look like a tree anymore. It looked like a beggar king dressed in the rags of a kingdom that had failed.

The lower branches were heavy with color. Not leaves—scraps. Thousands of them. Strips of blue wool torn from hem lines, lengths of dirty red linen, faded ribbons, and bandages stained with old rust. They were tied to every twig and protrusion within reach, fluttering in the biting wind with a sound like a thousand dry whispers.

Snap-hiss. Snap-hiss.

It wasn't a grave. It was a plea.

Nia stepped into the clearing. She wasn't alone.

A woman was kneeling in the mud at the base of the trunk. It was Sarai, the baker's wife. She was a hard woman, known for sharp elbows in the market and a tongue that could strip paint. But here, she was small. Her shoulders shook.

She was pressing a small, round object into the dirt between the massive roots. A hard tack biscuit, burnt black. An offering.

"Sarai," Nia said softly.

The woman flinched violently, scrambling back as if struck. When she saw it was only the midwife, she slumped, wiping her muddy hands on her apron.

"You startled me, Nia."

"What are you doing, Sarai?" Nia used the tip of her cane to point at the biscuit. "That is food. The flour is scarce."

"It's not food," Sarai whispered, looking at the black bark of the tree. "It's payment."

"Payment for what?"

"For listening." Sarai stood up, shivering. Her eyes were red-rimmed and hollow. "I lost my boy, Nia. The fever took him three nights ago. I prayed at the temple. I lit the candles. The stone gods didn't answer. They never answer."

She stepped closer to the tree, reaching out a hand but stopping short of touching it.

"But she listens," Sarai said, her voice dropping to a worshipful hush. "Can't you feel it? The air here... it's heavy. It holds you."

Nia felt a chill that had nothing to do with the wind. She looked at the tree—the metallic, teal-gray leaves hanging motionless while the ribbons danced.

"It is a tree, Sarai," Nia said firmly. "It is a grave for a girl who died because men were cruel. Do not make it magic. Magic is just a lie we tell ourselves when the truth hurts too much."

"Is it?" Sarai challenged. The grief in her eyes hardened into something brittle and fierce. "Then why is the snow melted?"

Nia looked down.

Sarai was right. The clearing was covered in a thin dusting of frost, but in a ten-foot circle around the trunk, the ground was bare. The mud was soft, unfrozen.

"Rot produces heat," Nia said, though the explanation tasted like ash. "Decomposition warms the soil."

"It's not rot," Sarai said. She leaned in, gripping Nia's arm with desperate strength. "I touched it, Nia. It hums. Like a cat purring in the dark. Like... like a furnace behind a closed door."

She let go and backed away, adjusting her shawl.

"You can call it wood if you want, Midwife. But when I talk to her, the silence doesn't feel empty. It feels like she's holding her breath."

Sarai turned and hurried down the path, leaving her burnt offering in the roots.

Nia stood alone in the wind. The ribbons snapped around her.

Snap-hiss.

She wanted to leave. She wanted to go back to her cottage and sharpen her knives and pretend the world was made of simple things like bone and gristle.

But she couldn't.

She walked to the tree. She removed her glove. Her hand trembled.

She pressed her bare palm against the black bark.

It wasn't the damp, clammy warmth of rotting wood. It was dry. It was radiant. It felt like touching the stone wall of a hearth on the other side of a roaring fire.

And Sarai was right. There was a vibration. It traveled up Nia's arm—a low, grinding frequency, like a heavy millstone turning deep, deep underground.

Creak.

Nia snatched her hand back. She stared at the canopy. One of the metallic leaves caught a stray beam of sunlight. It flared, blindingly bright, not like vegetable matter, but like polished copper.

"You aren't resting," Nia whispered to the tree, horror and hope warring in her chest. "You are working."

She looked at the ribbons. The desperation of Oakhaven hanging from every branch.

"They are feeding you," she realized. "They are feeding you their pain."

Nia backed away. She turned and fled down the path, her cane slipping in the mud. She didn't tell Kael. She didn't tell the town.

But that night, she locked her door and sat by her fire, listening to the wind scrape along the shutters. She knew the waiting wasn't over. The earth had accepted the girl, yes. But feeling that warm, metal pulse, Nia suspected the earth had no intention of keeping her forever.

Year Eight

The brambles were winning.

Kael stood by the southern ridge, his chest heaving. In the last four years the blackberry vines had grown thick and wild, heavy with thorns that seemed to harden like iron as they aged. He tried to pull a thick creeper across the gap, but his grip faltered.

His hands—once capable of crushing walnuts—trembled. The arthritis that had begun in his knuckles had settled deep into the bone.

"Here," a voice said.

Nia stepped up beside him. At twenty-four, she was lean and sharp-edged. She didn't ask for permission. She took the vine from his shaking hand. She didn't fight it; she twisted it, found the natural bend in the wood, and wove it seamlessly into the barrier.

Kael watched. He rubbed his aching wrist.

"You didn't wear the gauntlets," he noted.

"I don't need them," Nia said, stepping back to admire the wall. "If you move with the grain, the thorns don't cut."

Kael looked at his own hands—scarred, stiff, shaped by decades of fighting the wood. Then at hers—smooth, efficient, shaped by listening to it.

He slowly unbuckled the heavy leather gauntlets from his belt. They were stained black with sap and time. He held them out.

"They aren't for the thorns," Kael said softly. "They're for the weight. The ridge is heavy, Nia. It gets heavier every year."

Nia hesitated, then took the leather. It felt like accepting a crown.

"I'll hold it, Kael," she promised.

"For a while," he said, looking toward the silent, copper-leaved tree in the distance. "But I think... I think the woods are preparing for a different kind of gardener."

Chapter 13: The Engineer

Year Ten

The Iron Empire did not invade Oakhaven with a scream. It arrived with a ledger.

The Empire measured before it moved. Where other conquerors burned first and sorted later, the Iron Empire counted. Acres. Yield. Labor hours. Calories consumed against calories produced. A city was not an enemy to be broken but a system to be optimized.

Resistance was merely inefficiency that could be corrected.

Torian rode at the head of the column. He was thirty-five, a Centurion of the Third Legion. He didn't look like a conqueror; he looked like a surveyor. He wore gray steel that fit him like a second skin, and his saddlebags were filled not with loot, but with maps and charcoal.

The column stopped in the town square. Oakhaven was exactly as the reports described: gray, muddy, and starving. But it was not silent.

A scream cut through the damp air.

Torian turned his head. On the steps of the Governor's Hall—a stone building that was surprisingly well-maintained compared to the rotting hovels around it—a man was being beaten.

He was a farmer, thin as a rail, clutching a small sack of grain to his chest. Two guards in the crimson livery of the local Governor were kicking him.

"Tax is due, rat!" one guard shouted, bringing his boot down on the farmer's ribs. "Lord Vane does not run a charity!"

Torian watched. He didn't intervene. He observed.

He noted the farmer's malnutrition (ribs visible through the tunic). He noted the guards' equipment (expensive, polished, but wielded with sloppy, emotional violence). He noted the grain spilling from the sack—oats, likely seed stock.

"Waste," Torian whispered.

He kicked his horse forward. The beast, a heavy northern destrier, stepped heavily onto the cobblestones. The sound of sixty armored Legionaries moving in unison behind him silenced the square.

The guards stopped kicking. They looked up at the gray-clad soldiers.

"Who are you?" the lead guard demanded, hand drifting to his sword.

Torian didn't answer. He signaled his lieutenant. Two Legionaries dismounted, walked up the steps, and disarmed the Governor's guards with a terrifying, wordless efficiency. Snap. Twist. Drop.

Torian dismounted. He walked past the bleeding farmer. He bent down, pinched a few grains of the spilled oats between his gloved fingers, and inspected them.

"Seed," Torian said. "You are beating a man for his seed corn."

"It's the Governor's tithe!" the guard spat, though he was backing away.

Torian stood. "Get him," he said to his men. "Bring the Governor out."

Lord Vane did not come quietly. He was dragged out of his hall, wiping grease from his chin. He was a soft man, wrapped in velvet that cost more than the town earned in a year.

"What is the meaning of this?" Vane sputtered, his face flushing red. "I am the appointed Governor of this district! I have the King's seal!"

Torian looked at Vane. Then he looked at the starving town.

"The King is dead," Torian said calmly. "The Southern Capital fell three weeks ago. Did you not receive the raven?"

Vane blinked. The color drained from his face. "Dead?"

"The Iron Empire administers this territory now," Torian said. He pulled a slate from his belt. "I have audited your books, Vane. Your region produces forty tons of grain annually. Yet your population is starving. Why?"

"The winter was hard!" Vane stammered. "The peasants are lazy! I have to maintain the garrison..."

Torian walked up the steps. He pushed past Vane and entered the hall.

The hall smelled of roasted venison and perfumed oil. Torian didn't look at the tapestries or the gold plate. He walked straight to the heavy oak desk where the town ledgers lay open.

He flipped the pages, his finger tracing the columns of ink. Population: 2,400. Grain yield: 40 tons. Tax revenue: Gold.

"You keep excellent records of your coin, Vane," Torian said, his voice echoing in the quiet hall. He picked up a quill and scratched a calculation in the margin.

"But your biology is sloppy. A man digging a trench burns three thousand calories a day. A man starving on twelve hundred calories burns his own muscle." Torian looked up, his eyes cold and mathematical. "You aren't governing a town. You are dismantling an engine to burn the parts for warmth."

He slammed the ledger shut. Dust flew.

"Inefficient."

He returned a moment later, dragging a heavy sack of flour.

He threw it down the steps. It burst open in the mud, white dust pluming into the air.

"White flour," Torian noted. "Sifted. You lose thirty percent of the nutritional mass to make it white."

He looked at Vane with the cold curiosity of a man examining a broken gear.

"You are starving your workforce to eat cake."

"It is my right!" Vane shrieked, finding his courage in indignation. "I am the Lord!"

"You are a parasite," Torian corrected. "And parasites are inefficient."

Torian drew his sword. It was a short, heavy blade, designed for chopping.

The town held its breath. The farmer on the ground stopped moaning.

"This valley is a funnel," Torian announced to the square, his voice projecting clearly. "The soil is black. The water is plentiful. It is a machine designed to feed armies. But you have broken the machine, Vane. You have eaten the parts."

Vane scrambled backward. "I can pay you! I have gold in the cellar!"

"I don't want gold," Torian said, stepping forward. "I want calories."

He swung the sword.

It was not a duel. It was a liquidation.

Vane fell. The silence that followed was absolute.

Torian wiped his blade on Vane's velvet cloak. He sheathed it and turned to the crowd.

They stared at him with wide, terrified eyes. They expected him to loot the hall. They expected him to demand the gold.

Torian pointed to the granary doors.

"Open them," he ordered his men. "Distribute the stockpile. Two scoops per family. Today."

A gasp ran through the crowd. A woman began to weep.

Torian raised a hand.

"I am Centurion Torian," he announced. "From this day, the Temple Tax is abolished. The Governor's Tithe is abolished."

Cheers erupted—ragged, desperate cheers. Men fell to their knees. They looked at Torian as if he were a god of deliverance.

Torian waited for the noise to die down. He watched them with flat, unsmiling eyes.

"Instead," he continued, cutting through their joy like a frost, "you will pay the Labor Tax."

The cheering faltered.

"Every man, woman, and child able to walk will work. You will not work for your lords. You will work for the harvest."

He pointed to the marshy lowlands to the east. "Drain that swamp. Plant winter wheat."

He pointed to the rocky foothills. "Terrace those slopes. Plant root vegetables."

He pointed to the ruined smithy. "Fire the forge. We need plowshares, not swords."

"But we are hungry!" the farmer on the steps cried out, clutching his ribs. "We have no strength!"

"The Empire provides," Torian said. "You will eat two meals a day. You will have clean water. You will have medicine."

He rested his hand on the pommel of his sword.

"But in exchange, you belong to the schedule. You will produce. You will stockpile. And if I catch anyone stealing grain—even a single oat—I will hang them from the bridge."

He looked at the dead body of the Governor.

"I have removed the parasite," Torian said. "Now, the machine must run."

Year Twelve

The transformation was absolute.

Oakhaven ceased to be a village and became a machine. Machines required compliance, not loyalty. Torian understood this instinctively. Bells replaced conversation. Schedules replaced judgment.

When work was constant and exhaustion predictable, dissent lost its language. People stopped asking why and focused on when. Hunger had once driven them; now momentum did.

The fields ran because they had to. The smokehouses burned because the bell demanded it. Even rest was rationed, parceled out in measured hours that left no room for dreaming.

The body was maintained just well enough to return to function the next day.

Torian told himself this was mercy. And in a way, it was. No one starved. No one begged. The children grew taller, fed on the Empire's nutrient gruel.

But mercy delivered at scale lost its shape. It flattened everyone beneath it equally.

Torian walked the fields every morning. He didn't carry a whip; he carried a slate. He checked the irrigation channels. He inspected the grain silos that were rising like stone towers along the riverbank.

The people were no longer starving. They were fit, their muscles hard from labor. But their eyes were dead.

They moved with the rhythm of the bell. Wake. Work. Eat. Sleep.

Torian stopped by a group of men digging a new irrigation trench. Among them was the boy, Tom—now a young man. His hand bore a thick scar across the palm where a leaf had cut him years ago.

Tom dug with a rhythmic, furious intensity. He didn't look up.

"Depth?" Torian asked.

"Four feet, Centurion," Tom answered, his voice flat.

"Make it five," Torian said. "The winter runoff will be heavy."

"Yes, Centurion."

Torian walked on. He felt a strange hollowness. He had saved them from starvation. He had given them purpose. He had executed their oppressor on the steps of his own hall.

Why did they look at him as if he were the devil?

Year Fourteen

The Empire needed more than grain. It needed iron.

Geologists arrived in the spring. They tested the rock in the western foothills, miles below the hidden valley. They found veins of high-grade ore.

Torian ordered the opening of the mines.

The air inside the western shaft did not smell like Oakhaven. It smelled of crushed rock, wet iron, and the sour, ammonia tang of unwashed bodies sweating in the dark.

Torian walked down the main tunnel, his boots splashing in the shallow runoff. He held a lantern high, though the rhythm of the work guided him more than the light.

Clink. Grunt. Scrape. Clink. Grunt. Scrape.

It was a heartbeat.

He stopped at the junction where the new vein of ore had been exposed. Thirty men stood in a line, stripping the rock face. They were naked to the waist, their skin coated in a slurry of gray dust and sweat.

They were chained.

The chain was a heavy iron linkage that ran from ankle to ankle, leaving exactly thirty inches of slack between each man. It was not a tether to a wall; it was a tether to each other.

Torian watched them swing. They moved in unison. The man on the far left swung his pickaxe. A half-second later, the next man swung. The wave of motion rippled down the line, efficient and unbroken.

"It's too slow," a voice sneered from the shadows.

Marek, the captain of the mercenary guard, leaned against a support beam. He was picking his teeth with a sliver of wood, his lizard-like eyes bored. He wore his armor loosely, and he looked out of place in the precise geometry of the mine.

"You're babying them, Engineer," Marek said. "Put the whip to the flank. Speed them up."

Torian didn't look at the mercenary. He kept his eyes on the chain.

"If you whip the flank, the rhythm breaks. The man flinches. He misses the strike. The chain pulls the man next to him off balance. The line collapses."

"They're digging rocks, not dancing," Marek spat. He stepped forward, raising a gloved hand as if to shove the nearest miner.

"Touch him," Torian said, his voice dropping an octave, "and I will dock your company's pay for a month."

Marek froze. He sneered, but he lowered his hand. "You care too much about the livestock, Torian. They're just diggers. We have hundreds more in the pens."

"They are not diggers," Torian corrected, checking the slate in his hand. "They are calories converted into iron. And right now, this line is operating at ninety percent efficiency."

As if to prove his point, one of the miners near the center stumbled. Fatigue had caught him. His knees buckled.

In a normal mine, he would have fallen. The work would have stopped. The guards would have shouted.

Here, the chain caught him.

The tension on the iron links from the men on either side of him went taut instantly. They didn't stop swinging. Their momentum physically hauled the stumbling man back onto his feet. The rhythm dragged him forward, forcing his body to find the beat again.

Clink. Grunt. Scrape.

The miner gasped, found his footing, and swung his pick. The line had self-corrected.

112

Torian watched it with a cold, intellectual satisfaction. It was beautiful. It was cruel, yes—the man had no choice but to stand or be dragged—but it was perfect.

"See?" Torian whispered. "Individual weakness is absorbed by the collective. One moves, all move. Isolation is impossible."

Marek looked at the chain, then at Torian. He shook his head, spitting into the gray dust.

"You're a cold bastard, Torian. I'd rather you just beat them. At least pain is honest. This... this is turning men into gears."

"Gears don't panic," Torian said, making a mark on his slate. "Gears don't run when the enemy comes. And when the Darkness arrives, Marek, I don't need men. I need a machine that doesn't know how to break."

Year Fifteen

Torian stood on the newly reinforced walls of the Keep.

Below him, the granaries were overflowing. The smokehouses were full. The mines were churning out ore. Oakhaven was the most productive outpost in the sector.

"Production is up forty percent," his lieutenant reported, handing him a slate. "We have enough grain to feed a division for a year."

Torian nodded. He should have felt proud. He had taken a dying pit and turned it into a thriving fortress.

But he felt a coldness in his gut.

He looked up at the northern ridge, toward the hidden valley. He hadn't sent men up there. The maps said it was impassable, and the locals whispered it was cursed. Torian was a man of science, but he remembered the copper hair. He remembered the feeling of being watched.

He decided to leave the brambles alone. It was the one piece of chaos he allowed to exist.

He looked back at the town. The people were filing into the

mess hall for their evening meal. They were fed. They were warm.

"Cattle," Torian whispered to the wind. "I have raised cattle."

He realized then what he was doing. He wasn't saving them. He was fattening them. He was building a stockpile for a war that hadn't started yet.

He touched the scar on his jaw.

"Well, ghost," Torian muttered, looking at the distant ridge. "They aren't hungry anymore. But I don't think you'd call them free."

The Engineer had built a perfect machine. Now, he just had to wait for something to break it.

Chapter 14: The Drifters and the Dead

Year Fifteen

The order Torian had built was gray, hard, and perfect. It operated on the geometry of necessity: calories in, labor out, waste eliminated. But perfection is brittle. It holds only as long as every piece behaves as intended.

It cracked in late autumn: a cloud of dust on the southern road. By solstice, the crack had widened into a seam.

Torian stood on the gatehouse of the Keep. The wind was biting, carrying the first grit of winter. Beside him, his lieutenant, a young man named Hake (the son of the man Kael had broken years ago), squinted into the distance.

"Refugees?" Hake asked, hand resting on his crossbow.

Torian raised a brass spyglass. "No," he said, the word flat. "Too much steel."

Through the glass, the column resolved into a chaotic smear of blue and rust. There were three hundred of them. They rode heavy warhorses that looked as lean and hungry as the men on their backs. Their armor was a mismatched salvage of plate and mail, scoured bright by sand but dented by years of casual violence. Their banners were sun-bleached blue, tattered into strips that snapped like whips in the wind.

These were the Silver Pikes. Men who had fought in the Border Wars, realized the pay was better in banditry, and drifted north. They rode as if nothing waited behind them and nothing ahead could be worse.

The column halted before the closed gates. The silence that fell was heavy, broken only by the snorting of horses and the clatter of loose gear.

A rider separated from the pack. He was a massive man, wearing a breastplate that had clearly belonged to a nobleman once, though the crest had been filed off. He had a gold tooth that flashed when he grinned, and eyes like a lizard—unblinking and devoid of warmth.

"Open up!" the rider shouted. His voice was a gravel slide. "We are the Silver Pikes, and we are thirsty."

"State your business," Torian called down. He didn't shout; his voice was projected with the dry authority of the engineer.

"Business?" The rider laughed. "Survival is our business, gray-Coat. The South is burning. The Horde is eating the Borderlands. We rode ahead of the smoke." He gestured to the formidable walls of Oakhaven. "We need winter quarters. And ale. And grain."

Hake looked at Torian, his knuckles white on the crossbow. "Sir? They are bandits. If we let them in..."

Torian looked down at the three hundred armed men. He did the math instantly.

One hundred Legionaries. High ground. First volley kills half. The rest take the gate. Thirty dead. Maybe forty. Thirty I cannot replace.

And behind these bandits was the "Darkness"—the Horde. Reports put it at fifty thousand strong. When that wave hit, Torian would need every sword he could find, even the rusted ones.

Torian lowered the spyglass. It was a transaction. A terrible one, but efficient.

"We do not give charity," Torian called out. "This is a labor camp. If you want grain, you earn it."

The rider—Kaelen, the Silver Pikes' captain—spat on the wood of the gate. "We don't dig, engineer."

"No," Torian agreed. "You patrol. You ride the perimeter. You hunt the wolves. And when the snow comes, you guard the pass."

Kaelen considered this, his lizard eyes scanning the archers on the wall. He weighed the effort of a siege against the comfort of a warm barrack.

"And the ale?" Kaelen asked.

"Included," Torian said. "Open the gate!"

Hake stared at him. "Sir, you're letting the wolves into the fold."

"Better the wolves you pay than the wolves you fight," Torian muttered. "Let them in."

The Rot Sets In

The Silver Pikes did not integrate; they infested.

Torian quartered them in the old tannery district, downwind of the Keep, hoping the smell would keep them contained. It didn't.

They slipped into the cracks of the order Torian had built, widening them with laughter, drink, and casual cruelty. They carried a different gravity than the Legionaries. Where Torian's men moved with uniform restraint, the Pikes moved with appetite.

They took up space loudly, leaning into doorways, sitting where they were not invited, touching what did not belong to them.

In the mess hall, the "Rot" became visible.

It was evening. The miners were eating their ration—a dense, gray nutrient gruel—in silence. They ate quickly, heads down, eyes on their bowls.

Three Pikes sauntered in. They were drunk, smelling of sour wine and unwashed wool.

One of them, a man with a scar across his nose, stopped behind a young miner. He didn't speak. He just reached out and put a heavy, gauntleted hand on the miner's head.

He pushed.

The miner did not fight back. His body had learned what his mind no longer questioned.

The Pike laughed and pushed harder, forcing the man's face toward the bowl of gruel.

"Eat up, mole," the Pike jeered. "Dig deep."

A Legionary guard stood by the wall. He straightened, his hand drifting to his baton. This was a violation of the peace. This was disorder.

But he caught the eye of the other two Pikes. They were grinning, their hands resting loosely on the hilts of jagged daggers. They looked eager. They looked bored.

The Legionary hesitated. He did the math, just as Torian had. Is it worth the fight?

He looked away.

The Pike shoved the miner's face into the gruel. Laughter erupted—loud, jarring, and unchecked.

The machine still ran, but now something was grinding inside it, shedding metal filings into every joint. The miners learned a new lesson that night: The rules protected the work, but they did not protect the worker.

The End of Jace

Jace was thirty-six years old. He looked fifty.

He worked in the lower paddocks, shoveling manure. The limp Annajewel had given him twenty years ago had worsened, gnawing at his hip until he walked with a permanent, dragging shuffle. The pain was his only constant companion. It was the only thing that felt real.

He wasn't part of the Iron Order. He was too broken for the mines, too weak for the fields. He existed on the fringes, drinking potato spirits to numb the ache in his leg and the louder pain in his memory.

On the night of the Winter Solstice, the Silver Pikes threw a party.

Bonfires burned in the streets of the tannery district. A pig was roasting on a spit. Fat hissed into old tanbark and the street answered with smoke. Drunken laughter echoed off the stone walls of the Keep, a sound that mocked the silent, shivering town.

Jace sat behind the tavern, huddled in his thin, moth-eaten cloak. He watched the mercenaries through the cracks in the fence. He hated them.

They were what he had wanted to be—strong, feared, violent. They took what they wanted. They broke things and laughed.

A Pike stumbled out into the alley to relieve himself. He fumbled with his breeches, swaying.

He saw Jace huddled in the muck.

"What are you looking at, cripple?" the mercenary sneered.

Jace scrambled to get up, but his bad leg seized. He slipped in the mud. "Nothing. I'm... I'm looking at nothing."

The Pike grinned. It was a cruel expression, lit by the distant firelight. "You're right about that."

He stepped forward and kicked Jace.

It wasn't a fight. It was just a man with a heavy boot kicking a sack of wet laundry. The blow caught Jace in the ribs.

Crack.

Jace gasped, curling into a ball.

"Please," Jace whimpered, holding his hands up. "I'm nobody."

The mercenary laughed and kicked him again. Harder. "You're dirt. That's what you are. Dirt in the road."

The Pike finished his business, spat on Jace, and staggered back toward the warmth of the fire.

Jace lay there in the freezing mud. He wheezed, tasting copper.

He looked up at the sky. The stars were cold and distant, indifferent points of light that watched him bleed.

He thought of the alleyway, twenty years ago. He thought of

the girl with the copper hair.

He remembered the look in her eyes as he stood over her with the club. He had thought it was arrogance. He had thought she was looking down on him.

Now, lying in the filth, Jace realized the truth.

She hadn't looked at him with fear. She hadn't even looked at him with hate.

She had looked at him with pity.

She had seen this moment. She had seen that he was empty. That he had mistaken noise for substance and violence for weight. He had spent his life trying to be the boot, only to realize he had always been the dirt.

The cold worked its way through him. For the first time, he did not resist it. Resistance required belief that there was something left to defend.

He began to crawl.

He didn't crawl toward the tavern. He didn't crawl toward the infirmary. He crawled north. Toward the ridge.

He didn't know why. He just knew he couldn't die here, in the shadow of men who were exactly what he had tried to be.

He dragged himself through the frozen drainage ditch. His fingernails tore in the hard earth. His breath hitched in his chest, rattling like dry leaves.

He made it as far as the edge of the town, where the cobblestones gave way to the wild grass of the foothills.

The frost took him an hour later.

In his final delirium, the pain in his leg vanished. The mud turned white.

He saw the woods. He saw a flash of copper hair, bright as a new coin.

He saw the girl standing over him, holding a stick of ash wood. She wasn't angry. She was just waiting.

"I'm sorry," Jace whispered to the dark. The words formed a small cloud of steam that lingered for a second, then dissolved. "I'm so sorry."

The apology did not save him. It fixed nothing. But it named the truth at last.

His heart stopped.

Nia found him the next morning. She looked at the frozen, twisted body, half-covered in rime.

She looked back at the town, where the mercenaries were sleeping off their drunk. She looked up at the Keep, where Torian stood on his balcony, watching the machine he had built.

"The wolves are in the fold, Anna," Nia whispered, closing Jace's staring eyes. "And the shepherd is blind."

The Empty Chair

Nia left Jace in the frozen mud. She needed to wash the sight of him from her eyes. She needed the smell of pine and the warmth of the cabin. She needed Kael.

She climbed the ridge faster than usual, her heart hammering a warning against her ribs. The winter air felt thin, brittle, as if the sky itself were holding its breath.

When she opened the cabin door, the silence hit her first.

It wasn't the peaceful silence of the valley. It was the heavy, static silence of a clock that had stopped ticking.

Mara was sitting by the hearth. The fire had burned down to embers, casting a dull red glow across the room. She wasn't crying. She was holding Kael's hand.

Kael sat in his high-backed chair, facing the window that looked out toward the orchard. His head was tipped back, his mouth slightly open. The heavy wool blanket had slipped from his knees.

Nia stopped in the doorway. "Mara?"

Mara didn't look up. She smoothed the white hair back from

Kael's forehead with a tenderness that broke Nia's heart.

"He asked for the window," Mara whispered. "He wanted to see if the tree had changed."

Nia walked forward, her legs numb. She knelt beside the chair. Kael's face was pale, the deep lines of worry finally smoothed out by the cold. He didn't look like a warrior anymore. He looked like a man who had finally been given permission to rest.

"Did he… did he say anything?" Nia asked.

"He said the gate is holding," Mara said, her voice trembling for the first time. "He said you have the gauntlets."

Nia looked down at her belt, where the old, sap-stained leather hung.

She thought of Jace, frozen in the mud below—a man who died wanting to be a wolf. She looked at Kael—a man who died a shepherd.

The winter had taken them both in a single night. The violence and the protection. The threat and the shield.

Nia stood. She walked to the window and looked out at the Copper Tree, standing dark and silent in the twilight.

"We are alone, Mara," Nia said, the realization settling on her shoulders like a mantle of iron. "The men are gone. It is just us now."

Mara nodded, staring into the embers. "Then we must keep the fire," she said. "Until the spring."

Nia turned back to the chair. Kael's hand had slipped free of Mara's grasp, resting open on the armrest.

For the first time since she could remember, the ridge had no one watching it.

Chapter 15: The Powder Keg

Year Nineteen

The world did not end with a bang. It ended with a crowd. Crowds were louder than explosions.

They pressed, shuffled, argued, and waited, carrying their fear in bundles and carts. Each person believed they were fleeing something worse. Together, they became something worse. Movement without direction built heat. Pressure followed.

No one in Oakhaven had planned for this many bodies. Roads clogged. Wells soured. Tempers shortened. Hunger returned—not as absence, but as competition. The valley that had once fed itself now strained beneath the arithmetic of too many mouths.

Torian understood this kind of ending. Not destruction by force, but collapse by accumulation. When systems failed, they failed under weight.

And the weight was still arriving.

The fall of the Southern Pass was the breaking point. The "Darkness"—that nameless, hungry horde consuming the borderlands—pushed the population north like a tidal wave.

Oakhaven was the bottleneck.

People began to feel it before they understood it. The air itself seemed crowded, as if too many intentions were trying to occupy the same space. Men snapped at one another over nothing. Small arguments lingered too long. It felt less like fear and more like pressure—like standing too close to a cliff edge without realizing it.

They came in waves. First, the wealthy merchants in their carriages, paying exorbitant tolls to the Iron Legion guards. The guards noticed it then—how conversations stalled when certain figures passed, how eyes followed without knowing why. No orders were given, no banners raised, yet people adjusted their paths instinctively, clustering or parting as if guided by an unseen current. It wasn't command. It was gravity. Then the farmers, pushing handcarts piled with bedding.

Then came the broken steel — defeated soldiers.

These men carried defeat in their bodies. It showed in how they leaned, how they watched hands instead of faces. And yet—when they stopped moving, when the shouting dulled—there was a strange alignment, a brief stillness where eyes lifted together, as if waiting for something they could not name. It passed quickly. But it left a residue.

Torian stood on the battlements, watching the road.

"Who are they?" his lieutenant asked, pointing to a column of riders emerging from the dust.

They weren't refugees. They were soldiers. They wore the green tabards of the River Duchies, but their armor was dented, and their banners were wrapped in black cloth to hide their shame.

"The 7th Infantry," Torian said grimly. "Or what's left of them."

"Do we open the gate?"

Torian looked at the valley floor. It was already a shantytown of tents and cookfires. He had the Silver Pikes (unruly mercenaries), his own Iron Legion (exhausted occupiers), and now defeated regulars.

"If we close the gate, they will storm it," Torian said. "Let them in. But tell them they answer to me."

He knew it was a lie even as he said it. They wouldn't answer to him. They would answer to their hunger.

Hunger was the only authority that never lied.

It stripped rank from uniforms and loyalty from banners. Men who had marched under colors and oaths found that empty stomachs argued more persuasively than any commander. Promises made in warm rooms meant nothing when the body began to calculate how long it could last on nothing.

Torian felt the shift immediately. Orders still went out. Bells still rang. But compliance frayed at the edges. Men listened with one ear and scanned the crowd with the other, weighing faces for weakness. Discipline survived only where fear remained fresh.

What terrified Torian was not rebellion. Rebellion could be crushed. What spread now was something quieter—opportunism. Each man measuring how much he could carry before the collapse. Each man asking not who do I follow? but what can I take before this collapses?

Hunger did not need a leader.

It only needed time.

The Friction of Iron

Year Nineteen

The courtyard of the Keep was no longer a military parade ground. It was a slum built of tension and mud.

Torian stood on the low balcony overlooking the yard. The air smelled of wet wool, woodsmoke, and the copper tang of adrenaline. Below him, six armies were trying to occupy a space meant for one.

It was a map of hatred.

To the east, near the stables, the **Silver Pikes** gambled on overturned crates. They were loud, taking up space with the arrogance of men who knew they were being paid more than anyone else.

To the west, huddled under makeshift lean-tos against the wall, were the **Green Coats**. These were the remnants of the River Army—proud regulars who had been shattered by the Darkness in the south. They sharpened their swords in grim silence, watching the mercenaries with the burning contempt of professionals forced to bunk with thieves.

In the center, trudging through the slime with wheelbarrows of stone, were the **Miners**. They were the invisible gears of the machine, chained by habit if not by iron, keeping their heads down while the predators circled.

"It's going to break, sir," Hake whispered, standing at Torian's shoulder. "Look at them. They're looking for an excuse."

Torian gripped the stone railing. "We don't have enough space. We don't have enough food. And we have too much steel."

As if summoned by his worry, the spark landed.

A Green Coat lieutenant—a man named Vance, whose tabard

was stained but whose boots were polished—was walking toward the water trough.

A Pike, sprawling on a bale of hay, stretched his leg out. It looked accidental. It wasn't.

Vance tripped, stumbling into the mud.

The Pikes erupted in laughter. It was a jagged, ugly sound.

"Watch your step, soldier boy," the Pike sneered, flashing a gold tooth. "Ground's uneven when you're running away."

Vance scrambled to his feet. He didn't wipe the mud off. He drew his sword.

The sound of steel sliding against leather cut through the courtyard noise like a scream.

"Stand up," Vance hissed, the tip of his blade hovering inches from the mercenary's throat. "Stand up and say that again."

The courtyard froze.

It happened in ripples. The gambling stopped. The sharpening stones went silent. The miners lowered their wheelbarrows.

Every hand in the yard drifted to a hilt.

The Pike stood up slowly. He was grinning. "You want to dance, river-rat? I killed three of your kind over a card game in Oakhaven last week."

"You are filth," Vance spat. "You eat our grain while we starve. You take our coin while we bleed."

"We win," the Pike countered, drawing a serrated falchion. "That's the difference."

"Enough!"

Torian's voice boomed from the balcony. He vaulted over the railing, landing hard in the mud between them. He didn't draw his sword. He stood there, an engineer trying to stop a landslide with his hands.

"Sheathe your weapons!" Torian roared. "The enemy is *out there.*

The Darkness is two days march away. Every drop of blood you spill here is a gift to them!"

Vance didn't lower his sword. His eyes were wild, rimmed with red exhaustion. "These animals are not allies, Commander. They are parasites. They stole the winter blankets from my men. They raided the infirmary."

"And you occupy the dry quarters while we sleep in the stables!" the Pike shouted back.

Other men were stepping forward now. A circle was forming— Green Coats on one side, Pikes on the other. The Highlanders, posted on the walls, were watching, hefting their axes, waiting to see who looked weaker.

"We are all that is left!" Torian shouted, turning to face Vance. "Look around you, Major. There is no relief column coming. There is no King coming to save us. This—this mud, these walls, these thieves—this is the last stronghold. If we fight now, we die now."

Vance looked at Torian. He looked at the grinning Pike. He looked at his own shivering, starving men.

For a moment, Torian thought logic would hold. He thought the equation of survival would outweigh the emotion of pride.

He was wrong.

"Better to die clean," Vance whispered, "than to live with rot."

Vance lunged.

Torian moved instinctively, knocking Vance's blade aside with his gauntlet, but he was too slow to stop the chaos.

The Pike swung his falchion. It caught Vance on the shoulder— armor crunching, blood spraying.

The courtyard detonated.

It wasn't a duel anymore. It was a riot.

Green Coats charged. Pikes roared and met them. The brawl spilled over the invisible lines of the camp. Men who had nothing to do with the argument drew knives because the man next to them had drawn one.

"Stop!" Torian screamed, shoving men apart, but he was drowning in it.

He saw a Highlander smash a Pike with a shield. He saw a Miner get trampled in the mud, curling into a ball as armored boots stomped over him.

Torian drew his own sword, parrying a wild swing from a panicked Green Coat.

"Form up on me!" Torian bellowed to his Legionaries. "Shield wall! Separate them!"

But his voice was lost in the din of screaming men and clashing iron.

Torian stood in the center of the swirling melee, breathless, mud spattering his face. He watched a stable burn as a torch was knocked over. He watched men killing the only allies they had left in the world.

He realized then that his machine had truly failed. He had built walls of stone and stockpiles of grain, but he had forgotten to build a reason for them to stand together.

They were a pack of wolves trapped in a cage, tearing each other apart before the hunter even arrived.

And somewhere beneath them, the earth shifted.

Year Twenty

The snow began to fall in November. It covered the mud, but it couldn't bury the tension.

Reports arrived that the Darkness was crossing the wetlands. They would be here by spring.

Nia sat on the porch of her cottage—now crowded with two refugee families she had taken in. She watched the smoke rising from the Keep. She could hear the shouting of the soldiers drifting down from the walls.

"It's going to break," she whispered to herself. "Before the snow melts, they will kill each other."

The thought did not feel like prediction. It felt like recognition. As if the valley had already chosen its moment and was merely waiting for enough bodies to lean the same way. The pressure had shape now. Direction.

She grabbed her ash-wood cane. She needed air. She needed silence.

She began the long, painful climb up the northern ridge. The path was overgrown, but thousands of feet—orphans, mourners, pilgrims—had kept it visible over the years.

She reached the clearing.

The crowd of ribbons on the lower branches of the Copper Tree had grown into a tapestry. There were thousands of them now, fluttering in the cold wind. Offerings from a desperate people praying to a silent god.

Nia walked to the trunk. The heat radiating from it was intense tonight. It melted the snow in a ten-foot circle around the roots.

"We are full, Anna," Nia said, her voice cracking. "The valley is full. The silos are full. But we are empty of hope."

She leaned her forehead against the black bark.

"If you are coming," she wept, "come now. There is nothing left to save."

The Snap

It happened at midnight.

Torian was in the War Room, arguing with the captain of the Green Coats over ration allocations. The argument was heating up; hands were drifting toward daggers.

Then, the earth jumped.

It wasn't a sway. It was a sharp, vertical jolt, as if the mountain had been struck by a hammer.

The wine goblets on the table fell over. The map rolled off the desk.

"Earthquake?" the captain asked, bracing himself against the wall.

Torian ran to the window. He looked down at the town. The fires were still burning. The walls were standing.

Then he heard it.

CLANG.

It came from the north. It rolled down the valley like a shockwave. It was the sound of metal tearing.

The arguing captains stopped. The soldiers in the courtyard stopped. The refugees in the mud tents stopped.

CLANG.

Louder this time.

Nia, standing in the clearing, scrambled backward, falling into the slush.

The Copper Tree was vibrating. The black bark was splitting, revealing not white wood, but a blinding, internal heat. The sound wasn't coming from the sky. It was coming from the core.

The valley answered at last.

For years, pressure had been building in silence—hunger stacked on fear, fear compressed into ritual, ritual hardened into waiting. The Copper Tree had taken it all without bending, without signaling, without relief. Now the force inside it exceeded what even iron-hard wood could contain.

The vibration was not rage. It was release.

The ground shuddered as if recognizing a long-delayed correction. Steam burst from the fissures carrying the scent of hot metal and wet earth, an alchemy no forge should have known how to make. This was not destruction announcing itself. This was a seal breaking.

Those who felt it knew, without understanding, that something old had finished ripening.

And something heavier than war was about to step back into the world.

The ribbons tied to the branches caught fire. They didn't burn with orange flame; they burned with green, copper-salt fire.

The ground around the roots began to churn. The soil boiled.

CRACK.

The sound split the night. A fissure raced up the trunk, tearing the iron-hard wood apart.

Steam hissed out, screaming like a kettle.

Torian, watching from the Keep, felt the hair on his arms stand up. He grabbed the windowsill, his knuckles turning white.

"The mine," his lieutenant gasped. "Did the mine collapse?"

"No," Torian whispered, unable to look away from the green glow pulsing on the ridge. "The seed is opening."

In the clearing, the massive Oak groaned one last time. The trunk pulled apart.

Silence rushed back into the valley.

Nia lay in the mud, staring at the open husk of the tree. The steam cleared.

Chapter 16: The Daughter of the Root

The Clearing

The steam did not drift; it hissed, screaming out of the fissures in the trunk like a kettle left on a forge fire.

Nia lay in the mud where she had fallen. The heat radiating from the splitting Oak was physical—a dry, oven-like pressure that pushed against the winter cold, turning the slush around her into boiling gray water.

She couldn't breathe. She couldn't look away.

CRACK.

The sound was not wood splintering. It was the sound of a dam failing.

The massive trunk of the Oak tore open from root to crown. It didn't explode outward. It peeled back. The dark bark curled away like skin, revealing a hollow filled not with sap, but with blinding, white light.

Nia shielded her eyes, expecting to be burned.

But the light faded, settling into a soft, resonant glow.

A figure stepped out of the hollow.

She did not stumble. She did not hesitate. She stepped onto the grass with a heavy, wet thud that shook the ground under Nia's chest.

The space she left behind in the tree did not collapse. The Oak remained open, empty, and quiet—a husk that had finished its work.

Annajewel stood in the clearing.

The girl who had died twenty years ago was gone. In her place stood something that looked like it had been birthed by the forest itself to speak to the sky.

She was encased in a protective weave of pale roots and thick, living moss. It wrapped around her torso and limbs not like armor, but like a heavy, earthen swaddle—a chrysalis spun by the ground to keep a precious thing safe from the frost. The roots curled in elegant, natural patterns, blooming with small, white star-flowers at the joints.

Her face was unmasked, sharp and sculpted, possessing the polished sheen of river stone.

But it was her eyes that held the distance. They were not just green; they were deep and vast, holding a light that felt older than the valley—the cold, clear brilliance of stars seen from a high mountain.

And her hair. It was no longer the bright copper of a new coin. It hung in heavy, thick strands of oxidized teal—Aerugo—flecked with bronze that caught the twilight like a constellation map. It clinked softly as she moved, like wind chimes glistening with starlight.

She was a child of the soil and the sky, held together by gravity.

Annajewel tilted her head. Crack. The sound was like a branch snapping in frost.

She looked at her hands. They were coated in dark soil, the fingernails thick and black. She flexed them, watching the dirt crack along the knuckles.

"Gravity," she whispered. Her voice was warm, resonant. It sounded like the wind moving through a canyon. "I had forgotten the gravity."

She looked down at Nia.

Recognition came slowly, like a sunrise through fog. Annajewel didn't just see the gray hair or the wrinkles; she saw the weight of the years Nia had carried. She saw the vigil. She saw the grief.

Annajewel knelt. The movement was slow, tectonic. She reached out a hand—caked in dirt, warm as a fever—and touched Nia's cheek.

"You grew old, Nia," Annajewel said softly.

Nia trembled, leaning into the touch despite the heat. "You... you came back."

"I never left," Annajewel corrected. "I only went deeper."

"You died," Nia sobbed, the tears cutting clean tracks through the mud on her face. "I buried you. We dug the hole. We put the earth on you."

"The earth was hungry," Annajewel said. She looked at her own hand, marveling at the strength in the stiff fingers. "But it is full now."

She stood up. The movement sucked the air out of the clearing.

She turned her head toward the south, where the sky glowed orange with the distant fires of the Darkness. She took a deep breath, tasting the smoke on the wind. She tasted the fear of the valley. She tasted the iron of the mines.

"They are loud," she noted.

"Fifty thousand," Nia whispered, struggling to sit up. "They call it the Darkness. They are coming to eat the world, Anna."

Annajewel didn't flinch. Her eyes, swirling with that distant starlight, reflected the orange glow. They were not terrible; they were ancient, filled with the patience of a galaxy watching a firework.

"Do you have a knife?"

Nia blinked, confused. She fumbled at her belt, pulling out her small paring knife. "It's... it's dull. I use it for roots."

Annajewel took it. The small, rusted blade looked ridiculous in her large, earthen hand.

She reached back and gathered the heavy, metallic mass of her teal hair.

"It will catch in the wind," she said simply.

She began to saw. It didn't sound like hair being cut. It made a sound like scraping a blade through wire and dry bark.

Skree-snap. Skree-snap.

The heavy braid fell to the mud with a wet thud. It lay there like a coiled serpent, heavy and inert.

She shook her head, and the remaining hair flared out—a jagged halo of teal and bronze, crowning her like a nebula.

She handed the knife back to Nia.

"Stay here," Annajewel commanded. "Go to the cabin. Lock the door. Do not open it until the silence returns."

"Where are you going?" Nia cried, trying to stand but failing. "You can't go down there. There are thousands of them. They have iron. They have fire. You are just one girl!"

Annajewel turned toward the bramble gate—the masterpiece of thorns her father had woven to hide them so long ago.

"They have iron," she agreed, not looking back. "But I have the earth."

She began to walk. She didn't float; she advanced. Every step left a footprint that sank deep into the soil.

She walked straight into the wall of thorns.

She didn't turn sideways. She didn't suck in her breath.

SNAP.

The brambles shattered. Thorns that had once torn wool and skin snapped like dry glass against her protective husk. The living shoots bent aside, whipping away as if bowing to her passage.

She walked through the barrier Kael had built to keep the world out, and she destroyed it.

The time for hiding was over. The time for alignment had passed. This was the time for collision.

The Town

Oakhaven was dying loudly.

The tremor from the ridge had sent the panic into a frenzy. The main street was a bottleneck of screaming livestock, overturned carts, and refugees trying to claw their way north before the gates closed.

A Legion Centurion stood on a crate near the well, shouting orders that no one heard.

"Clear the road! Make way for the supply wagons!"

He struck a man with the shaft of his spear. The man fell, dragging a woman down with him. The mob surged, threatening to trample them both.

Then, the shadows at the edge of town shifted.

A figure walked down the center of the trade road. She walked against the flow of the refugees.

Thud. Thud. Thud.

The crowd parted. Not out of politeness, but out of a sudden, hushed stillness.

They did not scream. They did not run from her. As she passed, the panic evaporated, replaced by a strange, heavy gravity. People stopped pushing. Horses stopped rearing.

She stepped into the torchlight of the square.

The chaos didn't resolve; it aligned.

The Centurion turned. He looked at the woman covered in the weave of roots. He looked at the teal hair jaggedly framed against the dark sky like a crown of old stars. He looked at the mud streaked across her skin.

She didn't look like a monster. She looked like something they had all forgotten—a piece of the deep world walking on cobblestones. She was beautiful in the way a mountain range is beautiful: vast, undeniable, and utterly unconcerned with the smallness of men.

He leveled his spear. "Who are you?" he barked, though his voice wavered. "Get on your knees, woman! This is a military zone!"

Annajewel turned her head slowly. She didn't blink. Her eyes locked onto his, and the Centurion felt a weight settle in his stomach that had nothing to do with fear. It was awe.

"I have been on my knees," she said. Her voice wasn't loud, but it resonated off the stone buildings, drowning out the weeping of the crowd. "For twenty years."

She took a step toward him.

"Stay back!" the Centurion shouted, terrified by her calm. He drew his gladius, the steel gleaming in the torchlight. "I said stay back!"

Annajewel didn't stop. She didn't raise a hand to defend herself. She walked straight into the tip of the blade.

The crowd gasped.

The steel point touched the mat of roots covering her chest.

SKREEE.

It didn't pierce. It scraped. There was a sound of metal grinding on stone. Sparks flew.

Annajewel kept walking. Her momentum was irresistible.

The Centurion's eyes went wide. He pushed, bracing his arm, trying to drive the blade home. The sword bowed. It bent into a U-shape, the steel groaning under the impossible resistance of the earth itself.

PING.

The blade snapped. A shard of steel spun through the air, embedding itself in the wooden post of the well.

The Centurion stumbled backward, falling into the mud. He scrambled away from her on his hands and knees, clutching the broken hilt, staring at her chest.

There was no blood. There was not even a scratch on the root-covering.

Annajewel didn't look at him again. She looked at the families huddled by the wagons. She looked at the miners watching from behind the fences, their faces pressed to the wood.

They were staring at her, their mouths open. They felt it—the radiating warmth, the scent of fresh rain and deep soil. They felt the safety of her presence.

"Where is Torian?" she asked.

The name hung in the air, heavy and demanding.

"The Keep," a voice called out—a man holding a broken cart wheel, his face pale but his eyes full of wonder. "He is in the Keep. They are fighting."

Annajewel nodded. She looked up at the stone fortress looming over the town, where the sounds of the riot were echoing down the walls.

"Go home," she commanded the crowd. Her voice was gentle, a stark contrast to her earthen power. "Unpack your carts. Light your fires."

"But the Darkness," a woman cried out, clutching a baby. "They are coming!"

Annajewel looked south. She smiled, a small, grim curving of her lips. It was not a smile of war, but of reassurance—like a mother watching a storm she knows will not break the house.

"Let them come," she said. "I have slept a long time. And I have work to do."

She turned and began to walk up the steep, winding road toward the castle. She walked alone, a child of the stars and the soil rising up to meet the iron.

Chapter 17: The Lion's Den

The Keep of Oakhaven was not a castle; it was a cage.

It was built to keep things in as much as to keep enemies out. Stone corridors funneled movement. Narrow stairs forced obedience. Windows were slits, designed for arrows rather than light. Even the War Room, with its wide table and high ceiling, pressed inward once the doors were closed.

Torian had once admired this efficiency. Control depended on compression. People behaved predictably when space was denied to them.

Now the cage was full.

Men who trusted nothing stood shoulder to shoulder, armed and resentful, each convinced the others were the true threat. The walls that had promised safety only amplified the tension, turning every disagreement into a test of dominance.

When the doors opened, whatever entered would not be stepping into a fortress. It would be stepping into a trap.

Torian stood in the War Room. The map table was buried under conflicting reports. The air was thick with the smell of stale wine and unwashed men.

Around the table stood the captains of the fractured army: Kaelen of the Silver Pikes, picking his teeth with a dagger. Captain Hrolf of the Highlanders, his arms crossed over his chest. Major Vance of the Green Coats, looking at the others with sneering disdain.

"We don't have the grain for a six-month siege," Major Vance argued, slamming his hand on the table. "My men are eating gruel while the miners get full rations. It's unacceptable."

"The miners dig the stone that keeps these walls standing,

" Torian snapped. "They eat."

"They are slaves," Kaelen laughed, leaning back. "Let them starve. If the Darkness comes, throw them over the wall. Slows the enemy down."

Torian gripped the edge of the table. He was tired. He had built this machine to save the valley, but the machine was eating itself.

"The Darkness is two days away," Torian said, his voice low. "If we do not hold the gate—"

BOOM.

The heavy oak doors of the War Room swung open.

The room changed before anyone spoke. It wasn't fear—not yet—but orientation, like iron filings turning toward a magnet. Men who had been arguing seconds before found their weight shifting, their attention pulled forward without consent.

Annajewel stepped through the center.

As she crossed the threshold, the heavy, earthen husk that had protected her in the clearing began to fall away.

Chunks of dried moss and thick root-bark peeled from her shoulders and dropped to the stone floor with a soft, crumbling sound. It was like watching a butterfly shed a cocoon.

What remained underneath was not a monster. It was radiant — and solid.

She wore a simple tunic woven from pale, living fibers that shimmered like silk. Her skin was scrubbed clean of the mud, glowing with a faint, healthy flush.

Her hair—that heavy, oxidized teal Aerugo—hung loose around her face, flecked with bronze that caught the torchlight like a star map.

She didn't look clunky or earthen anymore. She looked clean. She looked like the first deep breath of spring after a long, suffocating winter.

Two Legion guards stumbled backward into the hallway, their

spears lowered. They didn't raise the alarm because they didn't feel threatened. They felt... relieved.

Annajewel walked in.

The room seemed to recalibrate around her. Torches guttered, not from wind, but as if the air itself had become still and sacred.

She brought the smell of the earth with her—not the damp rot of the swamp, but the clean, sharp scent of rain on dry soil.

She didn't look at the captains with anger. She looked at them with a profound, ancient sadness. She walked straight to the head of the table.

No one stood to block her path. Not Kaelen with his easy cruelty. Not Hrolf with his crossed arms.

Each man felt, without understanding why, that stepping into her way would be like trying to block the sunrise. It wasn't dangerous; it was just impossible.

She stopped at the head of the table.

Kaelen whistled. The sound rang too loud in the stillness, obscene in its casualness. It was a desperate attempt to prove he still mattered.

"Well now. The local entertainment?"

Annajewel turned her head slowly. She looked at the mercenary.

"You are Kaelen," she said. Her voice was no longer grinding stone. It was warm, clear, and uncomfortably intimate. "Leader of the Silver Pikes."

Kaelen's grin faltered. "Who's asking?"

"You are so tired, Kaelen," she said softly.

Kaelen blinked. The smirk vanished, replaced by a flash of confusion. "I'm not—"

"You have been running for ten years," she continued, her eyes searching his. "Running from the south. Running from the silence. You fill the quiet with noise and violence because you are terrified of what you might hear if you stop."

Kaelen stood up, his face flushing red. He drew his dagger. It was a reflex—a defense mechanism against the truth.

"Don't you talk to me about fear, witch," he snarled. "I'll cut that tongue out."

He lunged. It wasn't a lethal strike; it was a lash of pride.

Annajewel didn't back away, she didn't dodge.

She simply reached out and caught his wrist.

Her grip wasn't crushing. It was gentle. It was the way a mother catches the hand of a child acting out.

Kaelen froze. He looked at her hand on his wrist. He expected pain. He expected the crushing force of a monster.

Instead, he felt warmth. He felt a sudden, overwhelming sense of safety that he hadn't felt since he was a boy.

The fight drained out of him instantly. His arm went slack. The dagger slipped from his fingers and clattered to the floor.

"It is heavy," Annajewel whispered, releasing him. "Lay it down."

Kaelen sank back onto his stool, staring at his empty hands, trembling. He looked smaller. He looked human.

Annajewel turned to the others.

She looked at Hrolf. "You fight because you are angry."

She looked at Vance. "You fight because you are proud."

Then she looked at Torian.

Torian felt the breath leave his lungs. He recognized the eyes. They were the same dark eyes that had looked at him in the alleyway twenty years ago, now filled with the light of stars.

"You," Torian whispered. "The ghost."

"I am not a ghost, Torian," Annajewel said. She placed her clean hand on the map, her fingers resting on the black line of the approaching Horde. "And I am not a mouse."

"The gate was open," she said. "Wood does not bar the way of the root."

"They are coming," Torian said, his voice shaking. "Fifty thousand."

"I know," Annajewel replied.

"We are broken," Torian admitted, looking at the defeated captains. "These men... they hate each other more than the enemy."

Annajewel looked around the room. The captains were quiet now. The aggression had evaporated, replaced by the vulnerability she had exposed.

"They are scared," Annajewel said. "Fear makes men lonely. And lonely men fight poorly."

The truth of it settled through the room. No one argued.

She walked to the window that overlooked the courtyard. Below, thousands of soldiers and refugees were milling in the mud—a powder keg waiting for a spark.

"Open the armory, Torian," she commanded.

"The armory?" Torian asked. "For who? The Pikes have weapons."

Annajewel turned back to him. The light from the window caught the bronze flecks in her teal hair, making her look like a queen crowned in starlight.

"Not for the Pikes," she said. "For the miners. For the farmers. For the fathers."

"They are slaves," Vance scoffed, though the bite was gone from his voice. "They don't know how to destroy."

"No," Annajewel agreed. "But they know how to grow."

She looked at Torian, her eyes fierce and bright.

"Mercenaries fight for coin. Soldiers fight for victory. But a farmer fights for the harvest. A father fights for the future."

She gestured to the window.

"Those men understand protection, Torian. They understand

that you do not burn the field to save the barn. They are dedicated to life. And against the Darkness, that is the only weapon that matters."

Annajewel walked to the door.

"Assemble them in the courtyard," she said. "All of them. The Darkness is coming. It is time they met the Light."

She walked out, the heavy doors groaning shut behind her.

Torian watched her leave. He looked at Kaelen, who was still staring at his hands. He looked at the map of the hopeless battle to come.

For the first time in twenty years, the knots of anxiety in his chest loosened.

He realized he didn't have to be the one to hold the valley together anymore. He had just been keeping the seat warm.

"Sir?" his lieutenant asked, voice trembling. "Do we really open the armory? For the cattle?"

Torian looked at him. He remembered his own words from years ago: I have raised cattle.

He smiled, a grim, tired expression that finally reached his eyes.

"They aren't cattle, Lieutenant," Torian said softly. "Not anymore."

He gestured to the door where the Shepherd had vanished.

"They are the Gardeners. And the harvest is due."

The Mercy of the Pickaxe

The armory doors were thrown open, but the courtyard was already moving.

The rebellion had not been a battle; it had been a tidal wave.

The Miners, hardened by twenty years of swinging iron in the dark, had surged up the causeway. They didn't have swords yet. They had hammers, chisels, and the terrifying strength of men who had been treated like mules.

148

They had the remaining abusive guards cornered against the inner gate.

Torian stood on the balcony above, his knuckles white on the stone railing. He watched the geometry of what could be his own destruction.

There were fifty guards trapped below, surrounded by a thousand furious miners.

"They are going to tear them apart," Hake whispered, standing at Torian's shoulder. "It's going to be a massacre."

Down in the mud, the circle tightened.

A Centurion—a man named Crassus, who was known for using the lash on the chain gangs—had tripped. He lay in the slush, his helmet lost, his face pale with the realization that his authority had evaporated.

Standing over him was Thomas.

Thomas was a giant of a man, his skin stained permanently gray by ore dust. His back was a map of scar tissue. In his hands, he held a heavy mining pick, raised high above his head.

The iron point caught the torchlight, a rusted star ready to fall.

"Do it!" a miner screamed from the back of the crowd. "Break him, Thomas! Like he broke us!"

"Blood for blood!" another shouted.

Crassus curled into a ball, covering his head with his hands. He whimpered. It was a pathetic sound, stripping away the soldier to reveal the frightened animal underneath.

Thomas froze. His chest heaved like a bellows. He looked at the cowering man. He looked at the pickaxe in his hands.

For twenty years, Thomas had dreamed of this moment. He had rehearsed the swing in the dark tunnels. He had imagined the sound of the impact.

But looking at Crassus now—shivering, small, and defeated—Thomas didn't feel the triumph he expected. He felt a sudden, heavy exhaustion.

If I swing this, Thomas thought, I become the man holding the whip.

The silence stretched, tight as a bowstring.

Thomas groaned, a sound of frustration and release. He shifted his grip. He didn't bring the point down.

He brought the flat of the handle down, planting it in the mud with a dull thud.

"No," Thomas rumbled. His voice was deep, echoing off the stone walls.

The mob murmured, angry and confused. Some shouted again for blood, their voices cracking as certainty slipped. "He deserves it, Thomas!"

"He deserves to die!" Thomas agreed, turning to face his brothers. "But we deserve to live without blood on our hands."

He reached down. With a grip like a vice, he grabbed the Centurion by the breastplate and hauled him to his feet.

"Get out," Thomas growled, shoving Crassus toward the open gate of the barracks. "Get inside. Lock the door. And pray we don't change our minds."

Crassus didn't wait. He scrambled away, slipping in the mud, fleeing not from a fight, but from a pardon he didn't understand.

On the balcony, Torian let out a breath he hadn't realized he was holding.

The tension in the courtyard broke. The miners lowered their hammers. The screaming for blood died down into a low, confused grumbling, which slowly settled into a strange, quiet pride.

Torian turned his head. He looked toward the main archway, where Annajewel had been watching the judgment.

He stopped.

She stood there, illuminated by the torches. The heavy, earthen husk was gone, left behind in the War Room. She wore only the tunic of pale, living fibers, her arms bare to the cold.

She looked fragile amidst the armored men and the mud—a single stalk of wheat standing in a field of iron.

But she did not shiver. And she did not look away.

As the miners began to stack their weapons and help the wounded, Torian saw the light in her eyes intensify. It wasn't a magical flare. It was the look of a parent watching a child take a first, difficult step.

The air in the courtyard shifted. The metallic tang of blood and fear evaporated, replaced by the clean, sharp scent of rain.

She didn't force them, Torian realized. She just waited for them to remember who they were.

Annajewel caught his eye. She didn't smile. She simply nodded—a slow, human gesture of respect—and turned to look at the men who had saved themselves

Chapter 18: The Sermon of Iron

The courtyard of the Keep was a pit of mud and resentment.

Torian had sounded the assembly horn. Eight thousand men stood in the freezing drizzle.

They were segregated by hatred: The Iron Legion held the high ground near the gate, their armor gray and polished. The Silver Pikes and other mercenaries slouched near the stables, nursing hangovers and cleaning their fingernails with daggers.

The Miners and Farmers—the "Cattle"—huddled in the center.

They were unarmed, shivering in thin tunics, their faces streaked with soot and fear. They weren't looking at the enemy. They were looking at each other. A mercenary spat at a miner's feet. A Legionary shoved a farmer.

The air crackled with the potential for a riot.

Then, the heavy doors of the Keep opened.

Annajewel stepped out onto the stone landing overlooking the yard.

Torian stood behind her, his hand on his sword. He expected the usual reaction—confusion, jeering, perhaps a stone thrown from the back ranks.

But the silence that followed her was immediate.

She looked different in the daylight. The frost and earth that had clung to her upon her arrival were gone. She wore only the tunic of pale, living fibers, her arms bare to the biting wind.

She wore no armor. No roots covered her throat. No bark shielded her heart.

She stood completely exposed—a soft, human thing in a yard full of iron and hard edges.

Her teal hair, jagged and short, caught the gray light like oxidized copper. She shivered once—a small, involuntary reaction to the cold—but her posture did not break.

She didn't shout. She didn't pace. She simply stood still, an anchor in the storm.

"You are cold," she said.

Her voice was clear, resonant, carrying to the back of the courtyard without effort. It sounded like a bell struck underwater.

"You are hungry," she continued. "And you are afraid."

A murmur went through the crowd. Leaders didn't talk about fear. Leaders talked about glory.

"I do not ask you to die for me," she said, looking directly at the Silver Pikes, who had stopped their slouching.

"I ask you to live for something that matters. Deliver us from evil, maintain what's good and right"

She walked down the steps, moving into the mud among them.

The crowd parted. They saw her bare feet sinking into the freezing slush. They saw the goosebumps on her arms.

The vulnerability terrified them. It forced them to ask: If she is not afraid to stand here unprotected, why are we?

She stopped in front of a miner—Thomas, the giant who had spared the guard. She took his rough, scarred hand in hers.

"It is not for your lives you fight," she told them, turning in a slow circle, holding Thomas's hand like a lifeline.

"It is for the Light. The light of a fire in a warm house. The light of a child's face when he is not afraid." The Light that is you.

She smiled. It wasn't a warrior's grimace. It was a soft, breaking expression of pure humanity.

"I love you all," she whispered.

A tear leaked from her eye. It cut a clean track through the dust

154

on her cheek.

The fear in the yard broke. It dissolved into something heavier: Responsibility.

She wasn't a god demanding worship. She was a daughter asking for protection.

"Open the armory," Annajewel commanded.

This time, no one argued. The Legionaries moved. They threw open the heavy doors. They began passing out bundles of swords, shields, and pikes.

But they didn't just pile them up.

A mercenary from the Silver Pikes walked over to a miner. He didn't sneer. He handed the man a short sword.

"Keep the point up," the mercenary grunted, adjusting the miner's grip. "And stay behind my shield."

"Thank you," the miner whispered.

"Don't thank me," the mercenary said, nodding toward the woman in the white tunic who was walking among them. "Thank her."

The Breaking of Bread

Night fell, bringing a bitter wind that rattled the tiles of the Keep.

The courtyard had been transformed into a bivouac. Small fires dotted the darkness, casting long, dancing shadows against the walls. The segregation of the morning was gone; men sat where there was warmth, regardless of the color of their tabards.

Near the stables, Kaelen of the Silver Pikes sat on a crate, sharpening his dagger. His stomach growled, a hollow, cramping reminder that rations were low.

He reached into his pack and pulled out a loaf of hardtack— dense, dry bread that tasted of sawdust, but filled the belly.

He looked up. Sitting across the fire was Major Vance of the

Green Coats. The Major was shivering. His coat was threadbare, and his pride, usually so stiff, had wilted in the cold.

Kaelen hesitated. He looked at the bread. He looked at the man he had threatened to kill two days ago.

With a grunt, Kaelen snapped the hardtack in half.

"Catch," he muttered.

He tossed the piece across the fire. Vance caught it, surprised. He looked at the bread, then at the mercenary.

"Why?" Vance asked hoarsely.

"Dead men don't fight well," Kaelen said, taking a bite of his own share. "And tomorrow, I need you to hold the left flank."

Vance nodded slowly. "The left will hold," he promised. He took a bite.

From the shadows of the stable overhang, Torian watched them. He felt the shift in the air—the tension bleeding out, replaced by the grim solidarity of the condemned.

He turned his head to look further down the wall, where Annajewel was keeping vigil.

She was sitting on a stone bench, her knees drawn up to her chest for warmth. The pale tunic offered no protection against the dropping temperature.

Torian walked over to her. He took off his heavy wool cloak and draped it over her shoulders.

She didn't startle. She pulled the cloak tight, burying her face in the rough fabric for a moment.

"You're freezing," Torian whispered.

Annajewel looked up. Her eyes were lighter now, the dark earth tones flecked with the first hints of spring green.

"The frost is leaving the valley, Torian," she said softly. "It is safe to grow now."

Torian looked back at the fire where the mercenary and the

156

soldier were eating together.

"It's just bread, Anna," he said.

"No," she corrected, leaning her head back against the cold stone wall.

"It is a seed."

Chapter 19: The Red Rain

The sun did not rise over Oakhaven. It merely greased the horizon with a smear of bloody light, illuminating the nightmare that waited in the valley.

The Darkness had arrived.

They were not an army in the way the Iron Legion was an army. They were a geological event. Fifty thousand men—mercenaries, berserkers, and broken conscripts—filled the valley floor from the river to the ridge line.

They had no uniform. They carried torches, jagged iron, and the hunger that had eaten the south.

Torian stood on the ramparts. Beside him stood Kaelen of the Silver Pikes and Major Vance of the Green Coats.

"Thrice the amount," Vance whispered, his face pale. "Countless. It looks like the sea."

Torian looked at his own forces gathered in the courtyard below. Sixteen thousand men.

A mix of polished steel and dirty leather.

"Open the gates," Torian commanded.

"Sir?" Vance looked at him. "We have walls. We should make them bleed for the climb."

"If we stay behind the walls, they will starve us out in a week," Torian said. "Shepherd's orders. We meet them in the bottleneck. We hold the road."

The heavy timber gates groaned open.

The Song in the Dark

They didn't march out. They poured.

The Iron Legion took the front, locking their tall rectangular shields into a wall of gray steel. The Miners took the center, their pickaxes and hammers held high. The Silver Pikes and Green Coats took the flanks.

They formed a line across the valley floor, blocking the path to the town.

The enemy saw them. A roar went up from fifty thousand throats—a sound that shook the snow from the trees.

Archers on the enemy side drew their bows. The sky turned black.

Fear rippled through the defensive line. It was a physical thing, a cold tremor that threatened to shatter the formation before the first blow was struck. A young miner near the front dropped his hammer, his knees buckling.

Then, a sound rose from the center.

It started with Thomas, the miner who had spared the guard. He began to beat the handle of his pickaxe against his shield.

Thum-thum. Thum-thum.

It was the rhythm of the deep mines. The rhythm of work that does not end.

The miner next to him joined in. Then the mercenaries. Then the soldiers.

Thum-thum. Thum-thum.

A low, wordless hum rose from sixteen thousand throats. It wasn't a war cry. It was a harmony—a vibrating chord of defiance that pushed back against the roar of the Horde.

Torian rode down the line, checking the formation. He passed the center, where Annajewel stood.

He pulled his horse up short.

He hadn't looked at her since the night before, when she sat by the fire in Torian's cloak. But now, in the gray light of dawn, he saw what the women of the town had done.

She was not wearing armor. She was not encased in wood or roots.

She wore a simple, heavy tunic, stitched together by a hundred different hands.

It was a quilt of the valley. There were patches of rough gray wool from the miners' old cloaks. There were squares of faded red linen from the farmers' best tunics. There were strips of green velvet from a merchant's wife, and sturdy brown canvas from the grain sacks.

Nia and the others had sewn through the night, stitching their own lives together to clothe her.

She stood there, a human girl wrapped in the labor and love of her people. She looked incredibly small against the backdrop of the horde, but the colors of the tunic seemed to vibrate against the gray mud.

She looked up at Torian. Her eyes were clear, bright green—the only magic she needed.

She didn't say anything, but the look was clear: I am carrying them. Do not be afraid.

"Shields!" Torian bellowed, his voice steady.

The cloud of arrows fell. Clatter. Ping. Thud.

Men screamed. But the line did not break. The miners didn't flinch. The girl in the patchwork tunic held them fast.

Then, the collision.

The Horde charged. It wasn't a tactical maneuver; it was a stampede. They hit the shield wall with the force of a landslide.

CRUNCH.

The sound was deafening. It echoed off the valley walls like ringing bells. Swords struck shields. Axes struck helms.

The battle became a grinder.

Bodies fell as rain drops. The mud turned slick and red. The Red Rain fell without pause. It was impossible to tell who was winning.

The pile of corpses at the front line grew so high it became a rampart of flesh.

Torian fought until his arm was numb. He was covered in mud and blood, his shield splintered.

"Hold!" he screamed. "Maintain!"

And they did.

They fought like unsung heroes. Men who had been enemies a week ago—mercenaries and slaves—now died protecting each other.

Kaelen the mercenary slipped in the gore, a barbarian's axe descending toward his skull.

Major Vance, the Green Coat who had despised him, stepped in. Vance took the blow on his shield, shouting, "Get up, you filth! We aren't done!"

Kaelen scrambled up, driving his pike into the attacker. They stood back-to-back, the thief and the soldier, holding the flank.

In the center, the miners fought with the terrifying silence of the dark. They didn't shout. They swung their hammers with the rhythm of the song. Clang. Breath. Clang.

They were outnumbered three to one. Fatigue should have broken them hours ago. But they weren't fighting for their lives.

They were fighting for the girl in the patchwork dress who stood behind them, refusing to run.

The Silence

Night fell, and then morning came again. Sixteen hours of slaughter.

The Horde, broken by a defense they could not comprehend,

began to waver. They had expected cattle. They had found a wall.

As the sun crested the ridge, the enemy broke. They dropped their torches and fled south, a dissolving shadow.

The screaming stopped. The wind died in the valley.

Annajewel stood in the center of the field.

She was untouched. The battle had raged around her, a hurricane around an eye, but she had not raised a hand. She had simply witnessed it.

Torian watched, breathless, as she walked forward.

She looked fragile against the wreckage—cloth, skin, and bone where armor should have been. The patchwork tunic fluttered in the breeze—gray, red, green, brown. A flag of unity.

She turned her back on the fifty thousand fleeing enemies. It was an act of supreme trust.

She faced her defenders.

She looked at Kaelen. She looked at the miners. She looked at Torian.

"You are safe," she whispered. Her voice was no longer the grinding of stones; it was clear as rain.

Torian stared at her, his heart hammering against his ribs.

He wanted to tell her to put on armor. He wanted to tell her that the world was still sharp. But he couldn't speak.

The peace she radiated was absolute.

She smiled. It was the smile of a season that had finally won against the dark.

"It is finished," she said.

Then, the physics of war asserted itself.

Thwip.

It was a small sound. Insignificant. The sound of a new stalk snapping in a gale.

Annajewel jerked.

She didn't fly backward. She simply stiffened, her head snapping up in surprise.

Torian blinked. He saw the black feather fletching protruding from her chest, just below the collarbone, piercing the square of gray miner's wool over her heart.

It was a stark, ugly blemish against the love they had sewn for her.

For a heartbeat, the world refused to accept the image. The Spring had just arrived. It could not end.

Annajewel looked down. Her movement was slow, puzzled.

She reached up with a hand that shook. She touched the shaft of the arrow. Her fingers brushed the wetness spreading across the tunic.

It was red. Bright, oxygenated, human blood.

She looked up at Torian. Her eyes were wide, filled not with pain, but with a sudden, childlike confusion.

"Oh," she mouthed.

Her legs folded.

She didn't crash like a tree. She collapsed like a cut flower.

She sank to her knees, swayed once, and tipped sideways into the mud.

The silence that followed was not the silence of peace. It was the silence of a heart stopping.

The archer in the distance—a nameless, faceless straggler in the rocks—laughed. Just once. A sharp, mocking bark.

Torian stared at the empty space where the light had been. He stared at the small, colorful heap in the dirt.

The horror hit him before the grief.

She became human to save us, he thought, the realization tearing through him like a blade. She shed the power so we could find ours. And because she is human, she can die.

Then, the screaming started.

Chapter 20: The Ascension

The silence that followed the screaming was worse than the war.

The Horde was gone, a dark stain receding to the south, but no one watched them go. Sixteen thousand men stood frozen in the mud, staring at the small, colorful heap in the center of the valley.

The wind howled through the pass, pulling at the hem of the patchwork tunic—the gray wool, the red linen, the green velvet—now stained a unified, dark crimson.

Torian dropped his sword. It fell into the slush with a dull thud.

He walked forward. His legs felt heavy, as if the earth were trying to drag him down. He fell to his knees beside her.

Her eyes were closed. The teal hair, usually so full of static and life, lay flat against the mud. The arrow was still there, an ugly, final punctuation mark in the center of her chest.

"No," Torian whispered.

He reached out and scooped her up. She was impossibly light. It felt like holding a bundle of dry leaves rather than a human girl. He pulled her close, rocking back and forth, the tears cutting through the blood on his face.

Kaelen the mercenary dropped to his knees beside him. The giant miner, Thomas, knelt in the mud, bowing his head.

Then, a wail went up. It started low and rose into a keen of absolute despair. The men of Oakhaven wept. They had won the battle, but they had lost the reason for fighting.

They had thought she was invincible. They had forgotten that to be human is to be breakable.

Then, the wind changed.

It didn't blow from the north or the south. It seemed to exhale from the ground itself. The air grew suddenly warm, smelling not of iron and death, but of ozone and ozone—the scent of a storm clearing.

A voice was heard. It did not come from the clouds, and it did not come from the mountains. It resonated inside their chests, vibrating in the marrow of their bones.

"She fulfilled the task commanded."

Torian froze. He looked at Kaelen. The mercenary heard it too; his eyes were wide, looking around for the speaker.

"She was sent upon you," the Voice continued, sounding like the deep, resonant hum of the earth, "to teach you the difference between the Shadow and the Substance. The Season is complete."

Torian looked down at the girl in his arms.

Annajewel opened her eyes.

There was no gasp for air. There was no pain. Her eyes were not the eyes of a dying girl; they were the eyes of the night sky, deep and full of infinite, spinning light.

The wound in her chest did not close, but it ceased to bleed. The wound in her chest did not close, but it ceased to bleed. It no longer belonged to a body that needed keeping.

"Torian," she said. Her voice was strong, carrying to the edges of the valley.

"You are alive," Torian sobbed, clutching her tighter. "We need a healer! We need—"

"Hush," she said gently. She reached up and touched his face. Her hand was warm, but it felt insubstantial, like touching a beam of sunlight.

She looked past him, addressing the sixteen thousand men who had risen to their feet, staring in wonder.

"You thought I brought the Light with me," she said, smiling. "But I did not bring it."

She pointed to the miner, Thomas. She pointed to Kaelen. She pointed to the farmers holding their broken pikes.

"It is the Light that is you," she said. "The light of a fire in a warm house. The light of a child unafraid. I only cleared the weeds so you could see it."

She sat up. Torian tried to help her, but she moved with a gravity of her own.

"You were always good," she told them. "You had just disconnected from the root. But you are grafted now."

A cheer began to rise. It wasn't the roar of a victory; it was the sound of a dam breaking. It was a cheer of pure, unadulterated joy. They weren't cheering for a military victory. They were cheering because they realized the great secret: She isn't dying. She is just going home.

Annajewel stood up.

"My task is done," she said. "You are the Guardians now."

She spread her arms.

The wind kicked up, swirling around her. The teal hair whipped around her face, turning into a halo of bronze and verdigris.

She began to glow. It wasn't a blinding flash, but a soft, golden dissolution.

First, her hands turned to light, scattering like dandelion seeds in the wind. Then her face, smiling until the very end, broke apart into a thousand shimmering specks of dust that drifted upward toward the morning sun.

Torian reached out to catch her, but his hands closed on fabric.

She was gone.

Torian stood there, alone in the center of the cheering army. In his hands, he held the patchwork tunic.

It was empty. There was no body. There was no blood.

He held the gray wool of the miners, the red linen of the farmers, the green velvet of the merchants. He held the fabric of the valley.

He looked up at the sky, where the last motes of golden dust were disappearing into the blue.

He didn't weep. He felt a profound, solid strength settling into his chest—a foundation that would never crack again.

He looked at Kaelen. The mercenary was smiling, tears streaming down his face, his eyes fixed on the heavens.

"She isn't gone," Kaelen said, his voice filled with awe. "She's everywhere."

Torian folded the tunic reverently over his arm. He looked at his men. They weren't broken soldiers anymore. They were whole.

He remembered her final lesson.

Win the battle that is inside you, he thought, feeling the truth of it root deep in his soul. And keep the darkness from this land.

Torian drew his sword, not for war, but in salute. He raised it high, the steel catching the sun.

"For the Light!" he roared.

"FOR THE LIGHT!" sixteen thousand voices answered, shaking the mountains one last time.

The winter was over. Oakhaven had survived the night.

And in the garden of the valley, the first green shoots of spring began to push through the blood-soaked mud, reaching for the sun.

Epilogue: The Crown of Copper

Year Twenty-One (One Year Later)

The winter had been hard, but the spring was generous.

In the center of the valley battlefield, where the mud had once been stained red, a miracle had taken root. A perfect ring of copper-colored wildflowers had bloomed. They were a species no botanist had ever named—hardy, vibrant, and smelling faintly of iron and apples.

They grew in the shape of a crown.

Oakhaven had changed. It was not a paradise; paradises are soft, and this valley was still made of rock and work. But the heavy, suffocating gray that had choked the town for two decades was gone, washed away by the rain.

In the town square, the morning bell rang. It did not ring for labor quotas. It rang for the gathering.

Torian walked down the steps of the Keep. He wore no armor. His tunic was simple gray wool, and his hands, once stained with ink and blood, were calloused from the plow. He had traded the drafting of war machines for the drafting of irrigation canals.

He stopped by the blacksmith's forge. The fires were roaring, but the sharp clang-clang of sword-making was gone.

Kaelen, the former captain of the Silver Pikes, was holding a heavy iron chain with tongs. He looked older, his lizard eyes softened by peace and a good breakfast. He wasn't melting the iron down to destroy it; he was reshaping it.

"Still at it, Kaelen?" Torian asked.

Kaelen grinned, the gold tooth flashing. " Iron remembers," Kaelen said. "Takes heat to teach it something new." He struck the red-hot link with a hammer, flattening it into a blade for tilling the earth.

"The widow Mara needs a new gate hinge," Kaelen added, wiping soot from his forehead. "And the school needs a new bell."

"See to it," Torian nodded.

He walked on toward the market. The segregation of the past—Green Coats here, Miners there—had vanished so completely it was hard to remember where the lines had been drawn.

Near the well, a heavy cart laden with timber had ravaged a rut in the mud. The driver, an old farmer, struggled to push the wheel free.

There was no shouting. There was no demand for help.

Before the farmer could even wipe his brow, a man stepped out from the bakery line. He was a giant, his knuckles tattooed with the blue dust of the deep veins—a former miner. Beside him stepped a man in the faded, patched tunic of a Legionary.

Without a word, the miner took the left side of the cart, and the soldier took the right.

They didn't look at each other. They simply leaned in. The strength that had once dug ore and the discipline that had once held shields now moved in perfect unison.

The cart rolled free. The farmer nodded his thanks. The men dusted off their hands and returned to their morning, the act of service as natural as breathing.

Torian watched them, a lump in his throat. The Lesson holds, he thought. The iron has not just broken; it has healed.

He reached the orphanage. It was no longer a dormitory for child laborers. It was a school. The windows were open, and the sound of laughter spilled out into the street.

Nia sat on a wooden stool in the garden. She was old now, her hair completely white, her body bent like a winter branch. But her eyes were fierce, filled with the light of memory.

Gathered around her were thirty children. They sat in the grass, silent, rapt.

"Did she have a sword?" a small boy asked, his eyes wide.

"No," Nia said, her voice raspy but clear. "She did not need a sword. Swords are for men who are afraid. She carried something heavier."

"What did she carry?" a girl asked.

Nia smiled. She reached into her apron and pulled out a dried apple ring. She handed it to the girl.

"She carried the Truth," Nia said. "She knew that you are not hungry mouths to be fed. You are not hands to hold a shovel. You are lights."

Nia looked up and saw Torian standing at the gate. They shared a look—a silent communion of survivors who had seen the miracle.

"She shed her armor," Nia told the children, her voice dropping to a whisper. "She took off the iron. She took off the root. She became soft, so that we could become strong."

Torian turned away, his heart full.

He walked out of the town, past the healed fields where green wheat pushed through the dark soil, and up the winding path to the northern ridge.

The brambles were gone. The path was clear, lined with the strange copper flowers.

He reached the clearing.

The great Oak stood as it had for a year—silent, split down the middle, a blackened monument to the day the earth fought back.

Torian placed his hand on the bark. It was cold now. The heat was gone. The vibration had ceased.

"The work is done," he whispered to the tree.

He turned to leave. Then, he stopped.

At the base of the split trunk, pushing up through the blackened ruin of the roots, was a single green shoot.